THE DECEPTION REVEALED

MASON BAZLEY

Contents

PROLOGUE

Wet and cold. Lips pressed against mine, breathing into my lungs. I inhale and my lungs grow bigger. I breathe in water, which rises to the top. I'm being rolled onto my side to throw up the water while gagging and gasping. The chilly forest echoes with my coughing and gagging. For a brief while, my eyelids flutter open as I scan my hazy surroundings. My trembling body is caressed by ground-level fog. I'm confused. Lost. My back is being tapped while hands hold and shake me. Sleep is all I want to do. During the frantic silence, my breathing is harsh and shallow. Once more, despite my attempts to maintain focus on the brightness around me, nothing stays in my eyes. I can hear a voice, but I won't allow it to enter. Sleep. Just give me a bed." My face is lightly slapped while the voice cries angrily at me.

Everything suddenly goes dark once more.

CHAPTER 1

I have haze in my head. I open my eyes to fog. My head is killing me, thank God. My eyes begin to acclimatise, and I grunt, lifting a weighted hand to my head. I gasp and jerk, surveying my surroundings. Not at home here. I don't live here. Who am I?

In front of me, a window with frost. Is winter here? How long is winter currently? What the fuck is happening?

I wriggle the heavy blanket that is covering me as I sit up in bed. I set it aside so that I can see the obviously fake, oversized clothes I'm wearing. Jesus Christ, for real. I'm not a participant in some kind fan abduction, am I? God, please say no! I've encountered crazy fans before, and this would just be the icing on an extremely terrible cake. There is a downside to being a movie star.

I stare out the window while using my fist to remove the accumulated frost off the window's edges. Snow. Apart from all the bare trees—trees, I may add, that aren't palm trees—that's all I can see. I'm lost. Where am I? Nothing like the warmth of the sun touching my face every morning can be found here; this is not Malibu.

My recollections are hazy. It feels as if something is preventing me from recalling how I got here of all places. I loathe snow. Why on earth would I want to be here? However, Adrien had planned a ski trip to Alaska for the following week, didn't he? Last I saw, it was New Year's Eve. Or perhaps not.

I look around and grab the paper off the nightstand as my lower lip trembles. Talkeetna? What's there? The town's name doesn't hit me as strongly as what I see next. that day. 2 January. 2 days were lost! what took place to me?

I rip the paper to pieces. The local sheriff reports "teens smoking reefer by the ski lodge". "Causing havoc for locals" when a car strikes a moose on a major road. The entrance and exit boulevards are closed when it snows. This is insane. Alaska. I'm actually in Alaska.

I am aware of my identity and origins. But the enigma of what transpired to me during the past 48 hours stands alone. The ideas are coming in like sharp objects poking my skin.

After clearing my throat, I get out of bed. The enormous t-shirt has the insignia of a hockey team on it; as I don't follow sports, this orca-themed logo doesn't immediately come to mind.

When my feet come in contact with the chilly wood floors, the flannel pyjamas almost fall off of me. Everything is quite silent. I can hear my heart beating, goddammit. I disagree with this.

The dying fire hasn't received any attention in a while. I'm wondering who feeds the sweat as it trickles down my temples.

Clearly unoccupied for some time, the room has a cold, dusty feeling to it. Oh, how I wish my brain would function and remind me of what transpired the previous two days. It's got to be bad. No, it can't be something that will make me feel less anxious at this time.

I take in the cabin-like atmosphere as I scan the little space. I think the wooden bed was constructed by hand. also the nightstand. It has a peculiar carving on it that you don't typically see. The wall is covered with pictures, but my mind is too clouded to comprehend them. They seem hazy to me. I guess whatever knocked me out is still making me feel fuzzy. The idea of someone injecting me with a needle to keep me unconscious sends a chill down my spine.

As I look at the rustic stone fireplace with its wooden mantel, deer antlers, and strange cobweb stuck between the stones, my eyes start to flood up with tears. It makes me think of the time Adrien and I rented a cottage in the woods and spent the entire weekend screwing everything the property possessed. Similar to this fireplace, right down to the eerie antlers, was another fireplace.

When I notice another set of antlers hanging on the wall next to several empty picture frames, I take a deep breath and feel a shock wave through me. What makes them vacant?

When I consider glancing around the house, my heart tightens with fear. I'm here for a reason, don't you think? I'm rigid because of the unease coursing through me, yet I need to see beyond this place.

As I continue to stare at the door, my heart continues to beat quickly, filling my ears. What happens if this individual is a serial killer? What if they're a crazy fan holding me prisoner so they can wear my flesh as a bodysuit? Or even worse, what if they are? I think I might throw up. I believe I am moving too quickly. But because I'm a well-known actress and am wed to Bailey Industries' famed Adrien Bailey, I tend to draw people who are prone to psychosis. Just have a peek at me. Alaskan memory loss. I'm tense as hell.

I take a deep breath and re-wrap my pyjamas around my waist. When I consider what might have happened to me, I feel fear. I might have been abused and not even realised it. Drugs have caused mutilation and the absence of pain. No, no. I would undoubtedly notice that. Thinking about it is making me dizzy.

Lifting my trembling hand, I turn the doorknob. My body tenses when I peek into the corridor to discover that it is equally as gloomy as the chamber. The corridor, which leads to a staircase and has additional wood on the walls and flooring, is in the middle of a thin carpet with a pattern. It's vacant.

As the aroma of bacon drifts in my direction, my stomach begins to grumble loudly. Bacon has been eight years since I last ate it. Oh my god, the aroma is divine!

No, get back to reality. I have no recall of how I got here and I'm in a house I don't recognise wearing clothing that aren't mine. Bacon is not urgent.

My swallows get obstructed by a lump in my throat, and I start to whimper. I have no idea where I am or whose house this is. What if they're down there waiting? What if I am stabbed with a needle and go back to dreaming? terrible two days wasted. TWO! I wish to return home!

The sight of a baseball bat at the bottom of the stairs leaves me speechless with terror and makes me wonder why it is there in the first place. Okay, I have a couple of options.

1) I make a scene and create too much noise by lunging for it. If my captor sees me, he or she may throw me back into the chamber or worse. Behead me. No, hurt me as you record it like some crazy, sadistic a**hole.

2) Grab the bat and slowly down the stairs while keeping track of my whereabouts.

Option two. Move forward with that.

The wood flooring begins to creak and crack with each step I take, making it obvious that I'm moving around. I guess I'm not as stealthy as I thought.

Even if my heart is thumping furiously, the inevitable cannot be avoided. Even in the midst of the turmoil and worry, I have to know where the fuck I am.

As I descend the staircase, my breathing becomes shaky. The sound of bacon crinkling against the pan pierces my eardrum, and as I descend, warmth grows. Heat ought not to rise, right? Why is the upstairs area so freezing?

When I finally reach the bottom, loud barking startles me and makes me grab the handrail firmly enough for my nails to pierce the wood. The dog could be lunging at me, but I'm too preoccupied with the bat at my feet to check. No matter how rubbery my legs feel, I steady myself by wrapping my fingers over the handle.

A deep voice screams out, "Quiet down, Marlow," and a tense urgency swells in my chest.

When I look up, a man with dark hair and jade eyes smiles at me and prepares to look me in the eye. He can tell his age by the crinkle around them, for sure. He is likely in his mid-thirties. He has a thick beard that obscures his facial features and contours and is slightly lighter in colour than his hair. Hovering over the counter are his big shoulders. He definitely doesn't resemble a person you'd find in a kitchen.

When I take him in, my heart rate is on high alert. He is able to snap me with one hand while beating me with the other while grabbing the bat.

Oh my God, this place is killing me.

I feel a cold come over me as tears stream down my face. I am able to say, "H-hi," as I firmly grasp the bat.

I'm so terrified that when I start weeping, I can't help but keep crying. He has a taller posture, which makes me whimper. He can easily outclass my small frame. He'll be able to avoid it and easily tackle me with one stroke of the bat. I'm completely screwed.

He inquires, "How are you feeling?" I get chills from his voice because of how deep it is.

I have no idea what's happening to me or how I'm feeling. What sort of a query is that?

I inquire, scanning his dishevelled home. "Where am I?"

He whisks eggs in a bowl and pours them into a skillet, acting so eerily normal, "I'm assuming a long ways from home." His words cause panic to flow through my body and thud in my skull.

I expected him to be somewhat more sympathetic or even sympathetic and let me know where I was, what had happened to me, and how the fuck he had discovered me. Or did he believe that leaving me a newspaper would suffice as an answer?

As I look out the windows all around us, I try to control my breathing in an effort to reduce my anxiety. The rising sun's reflection causes snow to shimmer like stars as it licks the earth. I'm unable to believe how stunning it is. I feel as though my anxiety is holding me hostage as this excruciating dread consumes me.

I don't know who this man is, and fear is screaming inside of me; I may be kidnapped for all I know. Nevertheless, the gentleness of those jade-colored eyes provides me with the solutions I think I'm looking for. I've always been too trusting, and now here I am, watching him stir eggs, feeling my hold on the bat handle slipping.

I go on, "And where's that?"

He rolls over a few pieces of bacon and says, "Alaska. Found you while hunting with my girl, Marlow. You were floating in the water with nothing on you." The season is not ideal for skinny dipping.

Once more, I look out the window as I attempt to put together my journey from Malibu to Alaska. However, everything in my head is hazy and appears to be TV static.

When I turn my attention to the man who is laying bacon slices on a dish, my muscles stiffen up once again. I desire to move. My feet won't budge despite my repeated commands to do so. What in the world am I expected to do in this circumstance?

He adds, "I'm Silas, by the way," observing the recent tears that have been running down my cheeks.

I sigh nervously, "Um," I begin, wiping my bottom lip. Parker Bailey.

His guttural laugh makes my skin crawl as he says, "Yeah, I know." I've watched a few of your films.

All I can utter is a "Oh." My throat is tight with my heart in it. My palms are cold. But I have a calm mind. Is it his attractiveness that makes me feel at ease? I mean, hot guys can't be crazy killers, can they? Lord, Parker. How insane are you?

My hands were trembling in an unnatural rhythm, which caused the bat to tremble as well and crash against the railing.

He looks at me once more. Breakfast will be served soon, so please seat down.

Marlow briefly comes to mind. She resembles a hybrid German shepherd because of her all-black appearance with patches of brown and white hair, including one that resembles an eyepatch and is located around her right eye. She turns her head to face me and starts to speak. She appears to be grinning. She makes me think of my old dog, Barkley, a lovely golden retriever that I had when I was a child. Although that dog is long gone, she used to have those large, brown eyes and a head tilt similar to Marlow's when she gazed at me.

As I attempt to move ahead, my knees give way, sending a tingling through my body. How am I acting? Why do I approve of this? This fear appears to come in waves, and my speech is frozen and confused.

My hold on the bat is currently the only thing that is steady.

I tremble as I hesitantly walk over to the table. Additional huge windows look out over the front garden, which has some grass poking through the snow. More cut wood was added to the stacks of firewood that appeared to have fallen over and been left that way. Even though my head is going a mile per minute, all survival instincts are suppressed by my roaring stomach. This explains why in horror films the ditzy female is often the first victim.

I'm a vegan, but right now, who gives a shit? I'm famished.

I quickly scan the area, waiting for someone to appear around a corner and assault me. It's quiet though. Far too quiet. "Do you live here by yourself?"

Marlow lets out a small bark, and I hear myself saying, "Moved out here about six years ago from the city, a life, and a job I hated." She was discovered by me as I was scouring my land, and she has been with me ever since.

It's just him. That scares me for some reason. My throbbing migraine is taking over, obstructing my thoughts and clearing the hazy fear they were harbouring. Why on earth would someone decide to live alone and in the middle of nowhere? You have a psychopath, I tell you.

He puts additional bacon strips on a towel and grabs plates from a shelf behind him. "Where you found me, was there anything nearby that would explain what I was doing there?" I ask.

"That wouldn't make sense at all."

What even does that mean?

The emptiness swallows us. The serenity is disturbed by whistling winds. The rest is replaced by a crackling fire. Nothing about this makes sense. I feel as though I am drowning. Completely lost and out of control.

"What's the last thing you remember?" he asks when he finally makes eye contact with me.

The idea makes my skin itch. I put a hand on my head and remark, "I don't know.

Even though Silas is friendly, I still get uneasy when I enter his home. Three bear traps, two deer heads, a moose head, and several old-looking firearms are positioned throughout the room.

Despite how uncomfortable it makes me feel, my foolish feet manage to find a chair so I may eat. Sure, eat. Aside from this horrifying fear, the only thought that crosses my mind is that I need anything to stop my stomach from screaming.

At the opposite end of the table, a gun is laying there. It's broken, so I can't really utilise it. I doubt that I would be able to operate a gun. I notice a cloth and bullets as I examine more closely. How is it that when I walked into the kitchen, I didn't see any of this?

He looks at the bat in my hand as he offers me a plate of food. He points to the rifle and the bullets and says, "I'm not going to hurt you or anything." "Just cleaning them up is all."

That's not the question I want to ask, though: "Are you a hunter?" It's as though he understood what I was thinking.

Do you intend to murder me? That's what I intend to say, yes.

He sets his plate at the other end of the table and says, "I wouldn't label myself as one, but we hunt when the season permits for food for the town and ourselves."

At the other end of this table, a rifle is lazily resting. I'm unable to yell. I can just open my mouth; nevertheless, nothing is audible. My ability to speak has failed. As I process the truth of my predicament, more tears start to fall. Not at home here. Not a buddy, this. Surely this isn't genuine.

I scream while holding the bat up, "Why am I here?"

"I would tell you if I knew."

"How do I know you won't murder me?"

He collects utensils and sets a fork and knife next my plate, saying, "I saved your life." At the back of my mouth, a bitter taste develops that I find difficult to get rid of. I swallow more saliva when I take more gulps. It hurts. You'll need food, so eat.

Will I need it? what reason?

I slump into the chair as I feel dizzy. Maybe he is correct. Perhaps he tainted the food?

However, I must eat. Don't I? How am I even able to eat at this moment?

I keep thinking about lunging across the table at him while aiming the gun as I keep staring at it. It cannot significantly differ from the prop firearms I use at work. Only so much harm can be done by this bat.

I grit my teeth as I consider whether to keep the knife for protection while I gaze at it. I do. My fingers get white as I hold the knife on my lap after sliding it off the table.

He sits down with a heavy sigh and tosses Marlow one of the four slices of bread he has on his plate after laying two slices of bread with butter on my dish. We sit there awkwardly while the crackling fire takes over and envelops us. As I stare at the food in front of me, my stomach starts to grumble, and I start to wonder if a serial killer would prepare me a hearty breakfast.

Perhaps they would? I have no idea.

He looks at Marlow with raised eyebrows and then begins to eat. I get chills from the house's spooky silence. Even though I don't know or trust this man, I need to eat since I'm hungry. I slowly eat a slice of bacon while nibbling on it as if it were my first time ever. Adrien—shit, Adrien—is the reason I've been vegan for eight years. He must be so distraught over me.

I blot my mouth, swallow deeply, and choke back a whimper. Was I by myself?

I observed, "from what I saw."

He gives Marlow another piece of bread while removing the towel off the table and wiping the rifle's muzzle. Is he really going to shoot me? He'll behave similarly to Chapman, the assassin of John Lennon. Because of the celebrity he killed, he was widely reported.

As tears stream from my eyes, Silas senses that I am looking at the rifle and stops cleaning it.

He raises his hands and moves the rifle out of the path. When the metal scuffs against the hardwood table, my heart skips a beat. It's helpful. I now have the weapon by myself.

He notices that I've moved the knife in my hands from my lap to the table and moves his knife out of the way. Without saying anything, he lets me know that he has no malice. It's a beginning, but it doesn't make me feel any better. I have no idea what will.

I have no idea who he is, where my spouse is, or how I got here. Knowing that this day might very likely be my last makes my heart race.

CHAPTER 2

When I totally clear my plate, I notice that I have some more energy. Running will be simpler after eating than it will be while I'm weak. But I need responses. Something before I leave this place.

Whistling can be heard near the stove, and Silas gets up from his seat. Coffee is brewing, and I wish I could recall the last time I drank some freshly brewed coffee. Starbucks is my go-to, and instant is my preferred method, but freshly brewed? It could have been my last visit to Paris. perhaps Rome. No, Nice, France, without a doubt. We also have a coffee maker in the house, but I don't think we've used it since the week we bought it.

Silas divides the liquid into two mugs and brings one to me.

I respond, "Thank you," as I stare at the hot. dark liquid.

"Sugar? He's still standing next to me, asking, "Milk?

I object to how near he is. He might seize the bat I've left on the table or the knife I'm holding in my hand. ten moments. He only needed to do that to put everything to an end.

My hazel eyes meet his as I look up at him, and an uneasy feeling comes over me. That agonising fear is still present. He might have saved my life, but I have no idea who he is or whether he poses any danger. To put it mildly, he is frightening, and he is merely standing there asking if I would want cream or sugar.

Just sugar, I mumble. I'm not sure whether he can feel my anxiety, but he removes the sugar from the shelf, sets it beside me, and then slides a spoon on top before settling back into his chair. I ought to leave. That would be reasonable to do, after all. But I am immobile. I don't think I could go more than ten minutes in this weather since my legs feel like rubber. How in the world did I get here?You're invited to accompany me while I go into town for some supplies and other things. You can contact someone if you want to or whatever, but I don't have a phone out here and neither do the most of us on this side of the river. Pick up some clothes that fit you, perhaps.

I glance down at the baggy garment that envelops my petite frame. The shirt must be one of his, and the absurdly large trousers must be his as well. Then it occurs to me: Does that mean he saw me naked if I'm wearing these clothes and not my own? My cheeks get hot just thinking about it. Even though I've previously performed topless sex scenes in my films, I was paid to do so. I might add, generously compensated. But my God, am I ever mortified if some random stranger sees me naked.

I look up in terror as the tangled mass of anxiety begins to consume me. I take a drink of the coffee, "Y-yeah, okay." "Um, just where are we? such is the distance to the city."

"Talkeetna." Before meeting my eyes, he takes another sip of coffee and gives the knife in my hand another look. About two hours from Anchorage, a little town.

This is illogical.

Why don't you have a phone? I ask myself as my heart thumps against my ribs and I glance down at the trembling knife in my hands. Everyone now owns a phone.

He chews on some bacon and then cleans his lips with the palm of his hand. On this side of the river, there are no phone lines.

I'm expected to accept this, right? I'm still unsure if he is imprisoning me.

I have no idea who to call even if I find a phone. I have all of my contacts saved. I no longer have any numbers that I have committed to memory. Maybe Adrien's, but I'm not going to call him just yet. Recently, there has been some tension in our relationship, and I'm not sure why.

We were together nonstop for eight years, nearly five of which were spent married. Not a day goes by that we don't mess up. I like every second of his addiction to me. I was a nobody when we first met, on the edge of tears at yet another unsuccessful audition, and had only $20 to my name. The rain was drenching. I was miserable—cold, damp, depressed, and angry. I knew I was lost the moment I saw his smile. While waving for a taxi, every car that passed me simply splashed me. He stood next to me, protecting me from the rain with his umbrella. He was not required to do it. I continue to wonder why he did that. But he did, and I immediately wanted to kiss him. He gave me his business card as he flagged down a taxi. I'm Adrien Bailey. When I saw his name, I almost yelled. I was familiar with the Baileys. They managed Hollywood. He was someone, and I was eager to find out what kind of someone he was. We were already breathless and bare after a week. We cohabitated for a month before moving in. My image appeared on billboards within a year, and a diamond ring was put on my finger. I was overjoyed, completely in love, and his.

But now that I know all the awful guys he hangs out with, I'm not sure if I should call him. Silas, is he one of them? Is he using my presence as leverage against my spouse for whatever he did? There are numerous justifications for my imprisonment. I have to leave this place and look for solutions.

With her nails clicking across the wood floorboards, Marlow spreads down on her red and black checkered dog bed and moves towards the window. I observe her diligently gazing at absolutely nothing as I calm my racing thoughts. The sun is attempting to break through as the snow is thinning. Even though there isn't a single cloud in the sky that is blue, it certainly feels like a lovely day. Although I don't like snow, the way it sparkles makes me think of the shimmering waves I hear every morning.

What should calm my anxieties is not snow. It does, though. It has that fresh start feeling.

I have a pair of women's boots in your room, if you need them. With his mouth full of food, he continues, "And some clothes that might fit, too.

He doesn't live alone here, does he? Why does he dress like a woman? Assuming that I'm not his first victim, fear returns. What about me? Is he my saviour, then?

I keep looking at the rifle between us as my ideas start to fall apart. I have no idea where I am, and he has only been kind. I don't know what to think other than to wait and watch how things develop. Right? No. I'm not sure. I feel as though I'm going crazy and that this is all a weird dream.

He slams the coffee mug down on the table after gulping it down. Give you my jacket, please. Today is a chilly one outside.

Unsure of what to say, I only nod. I want to question him endlessly, but I don't know where to begin. Why, for instance, did he not take me to the hospital? or the police? My stomach is beginning to ache once more. The uneasy fear of something horrible about to happen rushes in like a black wave, choking me.

"How long have I been coming here?" I inquire while taking another sip of coffee.

It has been "two days." He stands to place his dish on the counter after wiping his lips on his sleeve.

I've been sleeping all this time, right? I'm hoping he knows more than he's letting on, but thus yet, nothing has occurred to me independently.

Sleeping intermittently. You refused to get up when I repeatedly tried to get you up for breakfast and a hot bath.

Something aches and turns sour inside of me. It seems as though a portion of my recollection has been completely lost. What kind of a scenario is this? The question "Have I seen a doctor?"

Doctor will be absent until Wednesday. I went into town the day I discovered you to call and invite Lenny. "Oh," I murmur gently. "He's the doctor." How can this village have just one doctor? One!

I still find it hard to believe I was absent for two days. How in the world did this happen to me?

I twitch my lower lip, but I quickly snap it shut to conceal my fear. What if Adrien experienced a negative event? What if his covert business partners finally got the better of him? I must quickly receive some responses.

He switches on the tap and rinses off his plate while I take a trembling breath and relax my hold on the knife. Was I by myself when you discovered me? While focusing on the serrated blade, I murmur.

Silas gestures towards a loveseat-side red door. The entrance beside the stairs upstairs or back there are the bathrooms.

Was I by myself when you discovered me? I add, getting up from the table.

He brings my coffee mug and plate to the counter. "Yes."

I move closer to the counter while biting my face until it bleeds while standing on the other side of it. What led you to me? Am I injured? Was anything around here? Is there a trace of how I got there? I don't want to put him in a difficult position. But I have to approach him to get his response.

He takes a deep breath in and lets it out gently. "When I found you, you weren't in the right frame of mind." His eyes briefly rest on me. "You were mumbling incoherent things," she said. He throws out the remaining coffee while clearing his throat and rinsing those off as well.

He ends his remarks there.

No, I don't use drugs. I've tried it previously. But not enough to make you unconscious for two whole days. I must track down Adrien. He must be equally alarmed as I am. What if he's hurt? Oh my God.

He walks away from the washbasin and gives me a sweet smile as he turns to face me. He puts one jacket on the table and grabs the other two from the hooks beside the door before donning a puffy vest. A few homes are located closer to the river. Perhaps you have a connection there who might explain why you were swimming in waters that were below freezing.

Tonguing the pimple on my cheek, I scoff. Did you consult others?

"No."

I reposition how I hold the knife. The question "Why the fuck not?"

He scowls and arches an eyebrow in irritation. "Parker, I know you're renowned. I want no trouble at all. Why you choose to leave yourself in the sea in minus thirty degree conditions is beyond me. However, it cannot be right.

"So why didn't you call the police?"

He exhales an indignant sigh and shakes his head. "This town's sheriff is not to be trusted. They won't even try to help; they'll just utilise you for who you are. If you know what's best for your protection, it's better if you keep away from them.

I whimper inaudibly and cover my mouth. It's Jesus. How am I expected to proceed? He opposes me calling the police. He opposes my going to the police. I've passed away. He will hang my head from the wall like the moose, the lovely, or whatever is hanging there. I ought to go to the police. It must be accomplished.

He clears his throat and zips up his waistcoat. I resist my increasing panic once more. I have an iron will. I've always been, which helps with my films. But my heart is pierced by this mounting horror.

Parker, you can accomplish this. Fright can wait.

I'll research the matter before I start screaming. Regardless of the tickle that is slowly but surely grabbing at the back of my throat. I'll clean up this mess I've gotten myself into.

Silas complains when putting his hat on. "Marlow and I will be in the front. Take as much time as necessary.

Marlow starts to pant and flail her tongue around as her mouth is wide and she is eager to get outside. When Barkley wanted to take a stroll, she used to follow a similar procedure. It was adorable. I long for a pet's companionship. Maybe Adrien and I can acquire a puppy when I figure out what the heck is going on. Of course, I'll need to ascertain the cause of why he's been so distant from me for the past two months. We'll buy ourselves a dog like Barkley once we've fixed everything. perhaps even have a child together. I require a break from acting. I only truly need it.

As the front door opens and closes, I move in the direction of the stairway and quickly locate the restroom. The only items in the medicine cabinet are deodorant and ear swabs. Toilet paper and additional shampoo bottles are kept in the cabinet beneath the sink. It's unclear to me exactly what I'm looking for. Yet I spy. I must investigate.

I do what needs to be done and return to the room where I woke up, looking in the closet and dresser for clothes. There are only a few sweaters, a few tank tops, and shorts. I take off the baggy t-shirt and put on the slightly too-large black tank top instead because it is much more comfortable than the t-shirt. I grab a pair of socks and tuck my feet into some boots that are clearly a size too small for me in the back of the wardrobe. Till we go to town, this will have to do. Harvard is written across the breast of the jumper that I take off the hanger. These must belong to someone he knows, or at the very least someone he has known in the past. Wearing someone else's attire makes me feel definitely out of place.

Okay. We're going into town to look for solutions. I'm ready to get into a car with someone who claims to have found me in Alaska's river while I was completely naked. I'm a fool for agreeing to this. What else am I expected to do, though? To call for assistance, I require a phone.

I descend the steps once more while flicking my hair over my head and running my fingers through it. As I reach for the jacket with a shaking hand and put it on, fear flutters in my stomach. Even though I feel like I'm floating in it due to its size, it is excellent. There are undertones of sandalwood as well as whisky and tobacco in the aroma. I would say that the fragrances were calming.

The knife is still tucked away in the sweater's pocket. I'm not sure what good it will do me, but knowing it's there gives me a sense of security.

It's time to learn the truth about a journey into town with a stranger that allegedly saved my life.

CHAPTER 3

When I step into the cold morning, a cold with dread sweeps through my body and the wind whips my hair around. There isn't anything around but naked trees spanning out for miles. We're truly alone out here and the thought of no one hearing me scream brings tears to my eyes. There's an axe lodged into a tree stump, glinting in the sunlight. One swing and I'm a goner.

It's easier to hide blood out here than it is to clean it off wooden floors.

Marlow barks, sending my heart into my throat, and runs for me as if she's going to attack me. I back into the door, hitting my head on the metal knocker. Before I can cover my face and absorb her blow, she drops a green tennis ball at my feet, staring at me.

"Oh," I say, a nervous grin spreading to my lips.

Silas jogs over from the side of the house. "You don't have to do that." His breath casts clouds around him as he looks me up and down and he fixes the toque on his head, watching me zip up the jacket. "Take it you didn't find anything that fit?"

I look down at the pajama pants. "No."

He jerks his head and leads us to his red pickup truck. I hesitate, looking around at the nothingness once more before letting the irrational part of my brain follow him.

Marlow runs toward Silas and hops into the backseat, sitting right in the middle with her tongue flopping out. Silas glances over at me when he's in the driver's seat, his eyes looking more blue than green in the brightness. The raw panic that's eating away at me seems to settle when he smiles softly and leans over to open my door. I'm not going to lie, the panic settles every time we lock eyes. My sex addiction is on overdrive right now because of that husky look about him. He's the type of attractive where he knows how good he looks but doesn't take advantage of it. Unlike Chester Billsworth—the blond from those superhero movies. I keep getting audition requests to be part of the franchise, but I'm skeptical. For one, he's an arrogant ass, and two, do I really want to be in a franchise?

I quickly look away, feeling out of place and uncomfortable as I climb in beside Silas. I'm not sure why I'm allowing myself to trust someone so easily. Especially someone who found me naked in the river, delusional and hypothermic.

Trust is a funny thing. I tend to trust people fairly easily, keeping them on short leashes, mind you. Everyone I meet in the industry is usually a lying scum bag or fucking cunt looking for fifteen minutes of fame with me. Except for Adrien. I trusted him before I said hello.

Yet here I am, trusting Silas because I don't know what else to do.

Silas drives down a long narrow path, trees rise high up on either side of us; some naked of their leaves, other pine trees leaving clouds of snow as we pass. The truck bounces around but manages to find its center as he pulls onto the main road. Everything is so grey and uninviting, the slush piles onto the sides of the road, and some collects in the middle. Even though not much snow has fallen, it's enough to add some dullness and dirtiness to what I imagine is a beautiful city.

"You remember where you're from?" he asks, breaking the silence.

"California," I respond, missing the salty smell of the air. Ugh, I hate winter.

He grips the steering wheel, focusing on the road. "Long ways away from California."

"I, um, I'm supposed to start filming here in a few weeks. We weren't supposed to be here until then...so, I don't know why I'm here." I shake my head as tears suddenly start welling in my eyes. All I remember is Adrien planning an Alaskan trip one week before filming for my birthday. Our flight was booked for January 3, filming was to start on January 15. Not now. I don't understand why I'm here now. "What happened to me?" I whisper, staring out the window.

I'm going crazy. That's what it is. I've worked myself to my limit and finally snapped, forgetting how I got here. My psychotic break. I knew it would happen. I didn't know it would come so soon. But it's here, isn't it? I'm living it.

The second the tears skim my cheeks, Silas takes notice, sighing. "Shit, hey." He hesitantly puts his hand out to me and touches my leg, but I jolt and move it away, wiping my eyes quickly.

I sniff, pressing my hands into the seat and easing as close to the door as possible. "I'm f-fine."

He swallows, bobbing that Adam's apple that's hidden behind this long, thick beard. "Might be something in town that can help you figure out what happened to you?"

"Like what? I don't even know how I got here. I can't remember anyone's phone number. I don't even know who the heck you are..." I pause and take a breath, trying to compose myself. "Sorry, this whole thing is...God, I don't even know what to think."

"I wish I could help—"

"You've done enough. I mean, you saved my life," I interrupt him, sighing as I wipe another tear sliding down my cheek.

Silas nods and keeps his attention on the bumpy road. "Wasn't going to let you die out there."

I'm still a bit groggy and all these bumps and swerves are making me nauseous. I'm not sore by any means, and there are no visible bruises or scratches on my arms or chest that would indicate I put up a fight. A thought creeps in that maybe whatever happened to me was done by someone I knew. Adrien is the only person that comes to mind. Where the fuck are you?

I gaze out the window, staring at the hollow and lonely-looking trees that are kissed by a dusting of snow. My head throbs at the thoughts that are swirling in my head, but the longer I stare out the window, the easier it is becoming to piece the blurred spots in my memory together.

There was a party at our house in Malibu, drinks were flowing, and hors d'oeuvres were being served. I remember being handed drink after drink from Adrien, feeling more alive after each one. He was drinking, too, so it wasn't like he was trying to get me drunk. The party was the usual bore of people fake laughing and drinking too much. But Adrien and I were finally connecting again. We screwed three times that day. A lot better than the stagnant sex we had weeks prior where I'd let him screw me without kisses or words exchanged, simply lying there and taking it.

But after my fifth champagne that night, I don't remember anything. There seem to be glimpses of my eyes fluttering open and seeing myself in a moving car, then my ears popping from lift-off. I remember feeling cold, always so cold. Other than that, it's all blank.

Silas pulls into a quaint little town, nodding at one of the locals who walk in front of his truck. Nerves strike me suddenly as I study the people who all seem to know each other. Their muted-colored snowsuits blend in with the muted town. Each holding a coffee as their breaths cloud around them making it look like they're out having a smoke.

Laughter spreads through those conversing outside the coffee shop, genuine smiles I haven't seen in years. I live within the rich social life where fake laughter and plastic smiles are always expressed. Nothing is ever genuine. But these locals seem happy and intrigued by each other. Friendship. This is what true friendship looks like. This isn't Holly-wood that's for sure.

Marlow barks, which startles me out of my trance.

"Jesus," I sigh under my breath.

"You'll get used to her. She's all bark and no bite, aren't you, girl?" Silas smiles as he scratches under Marlow's chin. He looks over at me and nods at the general store in front of us. "There's a phone by the cash you can use. Just tell people you're with me."

Silas opens the compartment between us and hands me a pair of aviators, then gets out of the truck. He knows who I am without making it awkward. The last thing I need is to get recognized, and I believe Silas knows this, too. At least until I know what happened to me. My fame could have gotten me into this predicament.

Plus, I could use a break from fame, just for a little. Once I figure out what happened, that's exactly what I'm going to do.

Marlow sits in his seat, huffing against the open window. I let out a breath and follow, folding my arms as the cold air sweeps through me. This town looks like a place Adrien and I visited about three years ago when he thought of purchasing a ski lodge we could rent out to tourists for some contin-ued income when I chose not to work on a film. He never realizes how taxing it is getting into character, memorizing scripts, and all the press afterward. I'm a mess when it's all done, always keeping pieces of my characters with me. My therapist told me I'm too much in my head and I should try shutting out my thoughts or writing them down. I don't like her very much, she proclaims I'm a sex addict. But the Xanax she prescribes is reason enough to keep seeing her.

I glance around as Silas opens the door and a bell chimes above him. This quaint little store reminds me of my childhood. A town I left so many years ago. Everyone knew everyone. No secrets were kept and no privacy was given. I hated it, and yet I'm in the industry where I can never go grocery shopping without the paparazzi creeping around the corner. I left for a chance to breathe, and now I'm suffocating right below the surface.

Holding the door for me, he points at the cash register and takes a free cart. "Take all the time you need."

"Wait," I start, my heart hammering in my chest. He stops and turns, raising his eyebrows for me to continue. "Um, y-you don't have to wait for me. I'm sure I-I'll sort all this out once I get someone on the phone."

He nods his head. "If that's what you want."

I gulp, fiddling with the sleeves of the jacket. "I'm not sure what I want right now, I just don't wanna put you out."

"You're not putting me out." He continues onward, fixing the toque on his head.

I push my lips together and adjust the glasses on my face as I stare at the phone by the cash register. Who the hell do I call? I have no idea what I'm doing here or how I got here in the first place.

I groan, wiping the back of my hand on my mouth. I don't know Silas or what he's capable of. But if I don't get ahold of anyone, he's the only warm place I can stay. Well, there's always the cops, but I have this gut feeling that I should listen to him when he said. Sheriff in this town is not to be trusted. They'll use you for who you are rather than try and help. It's better if you stay away from them if you know what's good for your safety.

Panic sets in, heating up my cheeks and bringing with it my racing heart. Silas...do I trust him? Do I allow myself to rely on my instincts alone rather than rationality?

I remind myself that I have no idea who he is. Or if he had anything to do with what happened to me. Better yet, why the hell does he has women's clothing in his house?

This is all too much. Sweat trickles at my temples followed by rippling fear that's making the bile rise. I'm going to be sick. Oh, shit, I'm legit going to be sick right now.

I dart out of the store and hurl in two separate goes. My heart feels like it's beating in my throat and knocking at my ears. This isn't a dream. I'm not losing my mind. This is real life. This is friggen real.

I wipe my mouth and spit once more, trembling as I straighten up. Okay, Parker. Go back inside and make a call.

I can do this. This is madness, but I can do this.

My toes are numb from the cold and in pain due to the lack of room in these boots, but I press forward, still unsure of who to call.

I smile at the gingerly woman who sits at the counter, reading a magazine. As quickly as the smile spreads to my lips, it leaves when I read the headline. Parker Bailey found dead by Husband on Monday Morning in Alaska. My face grows pale and a lump forms in my throat. I want to scream, I want to wail, I want to barf again, but I swallow it this time.

There is a picture of Adrien and me smiling brightly on the red carpet of my last film. I remember that sparkling forest green dress that hugged my hips and plunged low in the back. Adrien wore a royal blue suit with black lapels and a matching bowtie. I love it when he wears bowties.

I shake my head without realizing it, why am I so focused on the picture and not the fucking headline? "...found dead by husband..." How could he find me dead? I'm standing right here. Whose body did they find?

This isn't real. This isn't real. This isn't real.

My breath catches in my throat. People will recognize me in this town. It could be a good thing or a bad thing. A flip of a coin at this point. Am I safe? Am I in danger?

What the fuck is happening?

I snatch a copy of the magazine from the rack and flip to the article. "...vacationing at a rental cabin...break from fil ming...lost control...drank too much...drug overdose...Adrien Bailey tried to save her...performed CPR for thirty minutes before an ambulance and authorities arrived to pronounce her already dead...found in the river...Adrien Bailey has never been more devastated..." I stop reading, I can't read anymore because my hands are convulsing.

What is all this bullshit? We were at our freaking party in Malibu on Saturday. What the hell is going on?

I take a shaky breath, keeping the bile down, and shove the magazine under my arm. I clench and unclench my fists, taking a few deep breaths to relax my shaking hands. I have to call Adrien. I need answers.

I clear my throat, step over to the rotary phone, and turn it around to face me. "C-can I use this?" I ask the woman, hoping the bile remains simmering in my throat.

"If you're making a long-distance call, be sure to dial one first," the woman says without looking up.

"Thank you." I have no idea how to dial on this type of phone. I remember having a toy like this as a kid and playing with it when I pretended to be an office worker. My mother used to allow me to dress up with her costume jewelry and high heels and I used to pretend to be on the phone with important business clients. I did that for hours. I'd do anything to escape that religious jailhouse.

I make so many mistakes while dialing because of how much I'm shaking. I have to hang up the phone three times before I finally dial out the right number, and then realize I have to hang up again because I forgot to dial one. Christ, I'm terrified about what's going on. How did he find me dead? DEAD? I'm living and breathing and trying to dial his freaking number. What the hell is going on?

Waiting impatiently for him to answer as the line thrills, irritating my eardrum, I wonder what the hell he'll say. This better not be a hoax. A publicity stunt. This better not be his fault.

"Hello?" a woman with a Parisian accent answers, her voice eerily familiar.

I stammer, shaking my head. "I'm looking for Adrien."

"Who?"

"Adrien Bailey, I'm—" I nod, even though she can't see me. "Just tell him it's about Parker."

Silence spreads on the other end and the phone is immediately disconnected. I look at the receiver and dial the number again. After two rings, a voice I love so dearly, but now begin to wonder if it was all fake, answers. "Yeah?"

A deep shrill seeps up my spine. "Adrien?"

"Who is this?"

"Really?" I scoff, keeping my voice low. "What the fuck, Adrien? Dead? The tabloids say I'm fucking dead! What happened?"

His deep breaths spread through the receiver, and a deep, annoyed sigh follows after that. I don't even have to see his face to know he's squeezing his eyes shut in that way when he's thinking about the right thing to say.

"Call here again and I'll make sure you never see the light of day," he snarls.

"Don't hang up on me," I bark. My body tenses and I'm gripping the receiver so tightly that I'm scared I might toss it at the wall of cigarettes. "Explain why the fuck I was found half-dead in Talkeetna of all places—" I choke a sob back so angry I'm shivering and my stomach is tight.

How could he say something like this? He's my husband. We flew the moment we met.

"Adrien?"

The line goes dead.

When I try to call the number again, I'm not able to. Did he block this number? It's not even going to voicemail. What is Adrien up to?

I slam the receiver and the cashier looks at me. I put my hand up in apology trying to hold in my tears, but it's not working. I let out a shuddered breath and glance around, to see if I can find Silas. I feel so lost and out of place, needing something to hold on to, even though I don't know who he is. Why is this happening to me?

I don't understand what Adrien's deal is or why he would want me dead. We're madly in love, aren't we? These past few weeks aside, I think he still loves me. He asked me to marry him on our first date. I pretended I didn't hear him over the loud music at the club, and when he asked me again and got down on one knee, there was love in his eyes, wasn't there? Yes, we have money, and yes, there are weeks on end we don't see each other because I'm on set in another country or state, but nothing was ever truly wrong between us aside from our schedules never syncing.

I lift the receiver and dial a number I haven't used in nearly ten years. My hands don't shake as I dial. The phone thrills four times before going to voicemail and my voice cracks when I speak. "It's Parker, I, um, I need some help—I'll try you again when I can. I'm in Alaska, but, um, I'm—" I pause and see Silas turning the corner with a packed cart. "Don't believe the tabloids, and please don't believe Adrien, he's my husband. Was my husband? I don't know...I'll try you again when I can. I'm sorry...for everything."

Silas nods at me as I hang up the phone giving the cashier a shy grin. He adjusts his toque, then places a few bags of chips in the cart. "Get in touch with whoever you needed to?"

I sigh, keeping Adrien's betrayal a secret. "Not at all."

Silas spots the magazine on the stand and takes notice of the copy under my arm. "There's snow boots if you want, just down that way."

I place the magazine face down in the cart. "I don't have any money."

"Don't worry about it," Silas says, grinning.

"I can't do that—"

"Again, don't worry about it."

Those eyes of his bore into mine and I look away, trying to remember the last time someone did something nice for me out of the goodness of their heart. I think it was Adrien, maybe it was my close friend, Alexis? It was a surprise party for my twenty-third birthday almost four years ago. The house was fully decorated, our yard had tables and chairs for the guests, and the cake was taller than I was; a red velvet with cream cheese frosting. It was perfect, and that was probably the last time someone did something perfect for me and not for Parker Bailey, the actress. Everyone always uses me for who I am and what I own. Nothing is ever given to me for no reason.

"I'd feel really bad about it," I say, shrugging a shoulder.

"It's all right," Silas replies, smiling. "Consider it an I owe you."

I grin at this and look down, feeling entirely small and vulnerable for the first time in my life. He knows who I am and is still treating me with kindness and respect. I am as much of a stranger to him as he is to me.

Tears blur my vision as I fold my arms and nod. I don't know what to do with myself. I have no one. NO ONE! How does someone whose face is all over the place have no one? "Well, thank you."

"Not a problem at all," he repeats, watching as a tear rolls down my cheek. "C'mon, we should get you some clothes, too."

The cashier looks over at us, studying Silas like he is doing something he shouldn't do. I really hope no one recognizes me until I figure out what is going on.

I should go to the authorities, but the way Adrien spoke to me seemed like it will put me at greater risk than anything. Right? Gosh, I don't know what to do. What does one do in a situation like this?

Silas' tall physique is so different from what I'm used to. Adrien isn't a short man, by any means, but wearing high heels around him is difficult, to say the least. The moment I put heels on, we are almost the same height—especially if I wear my platforms.

Silas' dark beard hides most of his face, and his husky voice and Texas accent make everything he says sound demeaning. Watching him move through the aisles, I realize he isn't intimidating at all. He has this kindness and selflessness to him, something I want to get to know more than anything. I can't understand why. For all I know he is dangerous and is the reason I'm out here, yet here I am having these feelings similar to those I had when I first met Adrien in the rain. Trust.

I still have to keep my distance. Who am I to say Silas is a nice man or not? For all I know he could be in on whatever

Adrien has done to me. If Adrien did anything to me. Fuck, I'm so confused.

Here comes the bile again, I don't know how much longer I'll be able to remain as calm as I've been. I do know that one way or another, I'm on my own.

CHAPTER 4

Silas points at the boots on the shelf. "All right. What's your preference?"

I glance at the selection, truly not anything like the designer boots I'm used to but what choice do I have? "Anything that doesn't squash my toes."

He chuckles softly, leaning on the cart. "What's your size?"

I slide a box off the shelf and place them in the cart. "These are fine."

"Whatever else you need, don't be shy to pick up. I'll be at the back of the store getting cuts of meat," he adds, nodding at me.

I look over my shoulder at the racks of clothing, knowing I'll need something more than these pants I'm floating in. "Are you sure?"

"I am." He chuckles softly and cocks his head to the left. "Bathroom supplies are that way, clothes are behind you, and if there's any fruits or veggies you want that you don't see in the cart, grab those, too."

I push my lips together, truly appreciating his generosity. "Well, thanks."

"Meet you at the cash, yeah?"

I lick my lips and wonder where on earth I should start or if I should go home with him. There is a phone here, a place I can call continuously in the hopes that someone who cares about where I am or what happened to me will try to find a way to help me.

Death. That's a fucked-up thought. The fear that Adrien wants me dead keeps creeping up my spine. Just imagining what he had planned and why he brought me here to die. How did he fake it? Who the fuck did he kill in order to put their dead body in my place? If he had anything to do with it, that is.

That scares me the most. The dark side of Adrien's business. I never ask questions. He made me the person I am today. He brought fans to my name—my name is his, for fuck's sake. What am I to do now? I can't go back out into the world and call my husband out on his bluff. His con. I need to lay low and find out the end game before anything. Silas is going to be my safe house. Truthfully, if it wasn't for Silas, there would be no mystery to solve and no story to tell. I'd really be dead.

I grab a few shirts and pants from the very distasteful clothing section and hold them to my chest. I still feel lost and in a state of disillusionment, but I know I have to come back here every day in the hopes that someone will answer. I haven't spoken to my family in ten years. I don't even know how to begin to say sorry. But family is family. I'll call until I hear a familiar voice. And if no one answers, I'll keep calling until someone does. Until then, a cozy bed and warm house will be my waiting place. Hopefully, someone will come to my aid.

Someone will come, won't they?

A debate brews in my head about whether I should call the cops or not. But Adrien's dark side of the business might put us in jeopardy. I could be killed by making that call to the cops. He could be caught by me making that call, too. Or worse. Maybe all of this bullshit is a misunderstanding? If I call the cops, what if they think I'm a looney and put me in a nuthouse? I can't deal with that. No. I can't call the cops. Not yet. I have to speak with Adrien somehow. I need to know his truth.

I make my way to the toiletries section, grabbing a tooth-brush, deodorant, hair elastics, and mascara—my blond eye-lashes are not going to be left uncolored. I start making my way back to the cash like Silas asked, when I nearly bump into a woman and her son. "S-sorry."

She swats her hand and scrunches her nose at her son, looking up at me. "You spending the weekend skiing?" the woman asks, moving her cart forward.

I glance around for Silas but don't spot him. "N-no. I'm here visiting a friend."

The little boy grins at me and picks a chocolate bar, holding it with such pride I can't remember the last time I felt proud of something like that. And I'm an Oscar winner.

We forget how the simplest things in life used to make us happy, and as we grow up, the simplicity changes and grows into our own selfish desires and needs until nothing is sacred, until nothing is enough.

The woman studies the items in my arms. "Which friend?"

I don't see how that is any of her business, but when I look back again and see Silas turning the corner, the tension in my shoulders relaxes slightly. "Silas."

"That's good he's finally moving on." The woman smiles. "How long are you staying?"

I try to keep my head down as she speaks. Maybe she'll take the hint and leave me alone. But I don't think it's working. She smirks, eyeing him coming toward us.

"I rarely see him in town unless it's hunting season. Did you just get in? He's been in town twice in the last few days." She snaps her fingers at her son, ushering him forward so she can move to the cash register.

"I've been here for two days."

The woman nods with a smile. "That's good." The little boy has a huge smile on his face as he hands the cashier the chocolate bar. "Well, happy new year."

Silas clears his throat, stopping behind me with a shy grin. "Happy new year." He eyes the boy and there's this look in his eye. Is it pain? Sadness? I know nothing about him other than his love for his dog and his newfound look at life six years ago. Then it comes back to me, the women's clothing. I have to ask him about it when I feel comfortable enough to pry.

"I, um, I hope this is all okay?" I ask, breaking his stare at the little boy. Silas' eyes smile when he looks at me and nods. "Do you know them?"

"No," he snaps, not skipping a beat. He sounds upset. Snapping at me like I asked him something repulsive. When he looks up at my reddened face and lips set in a hard line, he exhales a breath. "Sort of. Everyone in town knows everyone but we know nothing about each other."

I want to press but drop it immediately by the twitch of his jaw. "Okay."

He doesn't say anything else, studying the items in my arms. He places our items on the counter, nodding his head for me to put my clothes in the pile. The woman at the cash smiles at him, eyeing me with curiosity. This is a small town all right. People will start talking quickly about Silas and the woman he's with. Maybe that's a good thing. Maybe knowing he's with someone will bring attention to me and help with the discovery of what the hell happened.

Being the center of attention is my biggest strength.

He grunts softly when he picks up a few of the bags as if there's a pain he's trying to hide. I take what I can carry and he strains to take the rest, pushing open the door and holding it for me with his foot. Not only is he straining to carry all the bags and holding the door for me, but he's also taking care of me out of the goodness of his heart. A stranger he found in the cold. I wish there were chivalrous people in this world like Silas.

Marlow barks at us, moving from the driver's seat to the passenger's, excited to see him. He winks at her and drops the bags into the bed of the truck before getting in. His striking green eyes appear to be glowing in the sunlight. He fascinates me in so many ways. I want to know his story. I want to know why the woman was happy that he was finally moving on. What does that even mean?

I climb into the truck and he backs out of the spot, waving at one of the guys outside the coffee shop before speeding off. "How're you feeling?"

"I'm okay," I reply, looking at my hands in my lap. My wedding ring is missing, there's a tan line where it used to reside. Whoever did this to me must've taken it. Or maybe Adrien did. It was his grandmother's after all.

He tightens his grip on the steering wheel. "That's good."

I clear my throat, adjusting the sunglasses on my face as he turns onto the main road. "I, uh, don't think I need to see a doctor," I add, sniffling. "I really do feel fine...do you think I should see one?" I glance at him. "You found me, right? Was I in that bad of shape?"

He wrinkles his chin and tilts his head to the side. "Do you feel off compared to your usual norm?"

"No, not at all. I'm just cold, but the weather will do that."

Silence spreads for a moment and he inhales sharply, tapping his fingers on his leg. "Mm," he mumbles, looking at me again. "I didn't mean to snap at you." I frown, crackling my knuckles. "I used to have a son about his age," he says, tonguing his cheek. Used to. The more this man speaks, the more intrigue swirls in my belly. "He would've been eleven now."

I bite my cheek. "What happened?"

"Car accident," is all he says and I stay quiet for the rest of the drive.

How can someone who lost everything be so calm and collected?

A weight drops on my chest. His life is none of my business, yet I have this urge to discover everything. And now I feel like I'm about to cry. My problem is shitty compared to what happened to him. Swallow that lump in your throat, Parker. Do. Not. Cry.

Silas pulls up to his house and gets out of the truck faster than he got in. The women's clothing must belong to his wife. Maybe ex-wife now. I like that there's a mystery about him. It's interesting and attractive. And I like that he's single. Fuck, why am I being so obsessive? He just confessed to losing his son!

Diagnosed sex addict, right.

Marlow growls softly, spotting the odd squirrel running amok. I'm starting to like her, she is gentle but protective and it seems like she has taken a liking to me. From experience, not all dogs give you their ball after first meeting you.

As silence consumes us, I watch the trees zooming by and think about the magazine. Parker Bailey found dead by Husband. I feel like I can't breathe. Everything is closing in. Everything isn't real. Everything makes me want to scream.

What on earth did Adrien get us into?

I take a breath, compose myself, and get out of the truck, sliding the sunglasses off my face. Marlow follows after me and runs to the woods to do her business as Silas takes a few bags from the bed of the truck.

I look up at the sun, close my eyes, and imagine myself to be home. Walking onto my back porch and letting the hot

Malibu sun kiss my cheeks. This is nothing like home, this is madness.

A friggen nightmare.

How am I going to figure this one out?

Silas grunts, lifting another bag, and watching me. My eyes slowly open to his as he holds my gaze for several seconds and exhales.

Tension has built, something that was there from the moment I woke up this morning, but if I'm to stay with him until all this bullshit is resolved, I have to break this building tension.

"I didn't mean to pry into your personal life," my voice trembles as I speak, his intimidating gaze has me shriveling. "I meant what I said, I don't have to stay here if I'm imposing...um..."

He doesn't say anything but keeps staring at me. I'm not sure if he's trying to come up with something to say, or if he's shocked that a movie star is in his front yard.

He takes another deep breath and places the bags down at his feet, scratching at his chin as he speaks. "What happened to you, Parker?"

The way he says my name sends shivers through me. "If I knew I wouldn't be here right now."

"Magazines said you died."

"Yep and from the conversation with my husband, he told me if I called him again I'd never see the light of day, yet according to the tabloids, he found me dead and performed CPR on me." Tears threaten to escape. "I don't know what happened to me any more than you do."

He lets out an aggravated breath. "Your husband, is he dangerous?"

"Yes."

He crossed his arms, tilting his head down. "Does he know where you are? That you're with me?"

I stammer, lower lip quivering. "No, he didn't give me the chance to say anything before he hung up and blocked the number."

Marlow barks twice as she runs from one end of the driveway to the next. Finding her ball in the snow and growling at it.

Silas looks back at her and rubs his chin on his shoulder. "What do you remember?"

I hug myself, furrowing my brows as I speak. 'We were having a New Year's Eve party at our home in Malibu. Adrien kept handing me champagne glasses. I must've had, maybe five, six? Next thing I remember is waking up in your bed." I shake my head, sniffling. "No...I remember waking up briefly and it was really cold. Adrien i-is taking off my dress, but then everything blacks out again." I take a breath, realizing I'm crying, and cover my face. "We were supposed to go skiing for my birthday. He said he rented a little place near the hill. But we weren't supposed to be in Anchorage until Thursday to celebrate my birthday on Friday with a day of skiing and massages."

No, stop crying. You don't know him and you're crying like a crazy person.

Silas sighs sympathetically. "It's all right."

I calm down and remove my hand from my face. "Where you found me, can I see it?"

"Mm," he agrees and picks the bags up again with a grunt.

I don't know what to make of this. He doesn't react. Doesn't seem too concerned, yet it bothers me that he's not worried about the unknown parts of my story.

Who is this man? And why do I trust him already?

*

After we silently unpack the things he purchased, I take the boots and adjust them on my feet giving my toes the relief they desperately need. As he's packing the fridge, I take a quick look around, feeling like I should've done this already, and realize there isn't a single photo of anyone on the walls. There are framed photos, sketches of the town, of a moose. But no family photos. My eerie curiosity wants to see photos of his son, his wife, and what Silas looks like without the rugged lumberjack thing he has going on.

Silas drops the toiletries on the table in front of me with a grin, startling me. "Oh, God," I say, placing a hand on my chest.

He chuckles. "You scare too easy."

I smile, swallowing thickly. "My mom used to always say I was scared of my own shadow."

"And yet you make scary movies," he says, kicking the chair out beside me to sit down.

I fight a rising panic and dive my hand into my pocket to hold the knife. "Key to being a great actor is putting yourself in the character's shoes, right?" It's easy to talk to him, very easy. It shouldn't be this easy. How can I begin a simple conversation with all this chaos going on?

I sigh and shake my head. "How the fuck did they pronounce me dead?"

"What did your husband say when you spoke to him?"

I sniff, wiping an escaping tear. "He didn't say anything. He wasn't even concerned or happy to hear my voice."

Silas puts his hand out to me, retracting it almost as quickly as his palm faces upward. "You think he had anything to do with whatever happened to you?"

I fight back more tears, feeling my throat clog up. I need to breathe. I can't take this anymore. "What do you think is going on?" I rub the weight pressing harder on my chest.

He shrugs, sighing softly. "Your husband ever say anything to you about his business?"

"I stay out of it," I scoff and wipe the wetness under my eyes. "Come to think of it, I stay away from it so that bullshit like what's happening to me now, won't happen." I gulp down the lump in my throat. "How can the world believe me to be dead? Adrien found my body and did CPR. How can—fuck." I cover my face as more tears fall. "Who did they find?"

"You can't contact him again."

I sniff and remove my hands. "Why?"

His face grows serious, and the lines between his eyes deepen. "He may come back and finish the job."

I shake my head quickly. "He's my husband. This has got to be a misunderstanding. He wouldn't do this to me—"

"Parker, the world thinks you're dead."

I want to give my husband the benefit of the doubt. I should give it to him. But his words begin to cloud my thoughts. Call here again and I'll make sure you never see the light of day. What do you want, Adrien? Why the hell did you do this to me?

I sniff, whimpering softly. "Did you look through the magazine?"

He shakes his head, tapping his fingers on the table. The gun he was cleaning is just out of reach and a chill licks down my spine. He notices my fright because he removes his hand from the table.

His eyes jump to my lips, then back to my eyes. "I got some stuff to do 'round the house. Mind if we check the river out after lunch?"

"How many guns do you have around the house?"

"Not a one."

I don't believe him. "You have one right here."

"Not more than one."

Dread prickles my skin. "If you're going to kill me, please do it already. I don't want to live in fear—"

"I ain't gonna kill you, Parker."

"You gonna use me for my money?"

He lets out a nasal chuckle and slowly licks his lips. I shouldn't be attracted to the man who may have kidnapped me, but all I keep thinking about is what those lips taste like. I've gone mad, it's official. Parker Bailey has lost her mind.

"You can freshen up." His eyes slide to my hand in the hoodie that contains the knife. "If you want a bigger one, top drawer in the kitchen you'll find a few."

Is he mocking me? I haven't gotten a concrete answer out of him and he's mocking me like he knows I'm too scared to even try anything.

I suck my tear and remove my hand from the sweater pocket. "I was gonna take a shower anyway."

"Knob's a little finicky for hot water. Just wiggle it if the water starts getting cold," he responds, tapping the table. "Towels are in the hallway closet." He starts for the front door and stops. "I'll be out front if you need anything."

I nod and hesitantly escape to the washroom upstairs, looking over my shoulder at the top drawer in the kitchen. I take the toiletries but completely forget about the clothes. I'm not worried about it now, all I want to do is bathe as if my fear will dissipate like a whisp of breath on this cold day, knowing I can relax under the falling water.

He wasn't lying when he said the hot water knob is busted. I've jiggled it six times so far. But when the hot water falls on me, I'm not in a random cabin with some stranger. I'm home. I'm safe. Adrien isn't the one I believe tried to kill me. He's my husband and he loves me. He wouldn't break us. This is a dream. It's a stupid dream I'll wake up from.

Then the water gets cold and I realize this isn't a dream. I'm in a cabin with a stranger and it's friggen terrifying.

Glimpses of things come back to me. I'm not sure if they're real or if they're just glimpses of what my mind is making up because of the article I skimmed through. Drank too much...drug overdose...dancing naked by the river—I don't get blackout drunk. That isn't me.

Why did I buy that stupid magazine in the first place?

I keep seeing myself walking freely to the water's edge. My feet are frozen, but it doesn't seem to bother me since I'm dancing like no one's watching. I'm not myself, that's clear, but I don't go in the water. Adrien is there, laughing, smiling, and taking pictures of me like he usually does, then sells to the magazines for stupid amounts of money. Something tells me these photos won't be released until his so-called "grieving" is over. I see him, lying on top of me, his face is serious like he is about to do something he doesn't want to do. His lips touch mine for several seconds and the next thing I remember, everything is cold and dark. It's always dark.

I shudder, feeling the water turn cold again, and jiggle the knob one last time before I step out. Why, Adrien? Why did you do this to me?

I wrap the towel around me and start brushing my hair—knock, knock.

I jump, scrambling for the knife. "Fuck."

"Just wanted to let you know I put your clothes in your room," Silas says on the other side of the translucent door. "Added a few logs to the fire, too."

"Oh, thanks," I reply, wringing my hair out and opening the door. I hear him start for the stairs before I open the door and he steps back up, his hands in his pockets.

He eyes me for a moment, eyes downcast when I tighten the towel around me. "Don't read the magazine." Tapping the wall beside him, he jogs back down the stairs and leaves me with more weight pressing down on my chest. What does it say in the magazine that I shouldn't read?

I take a shuddered breath and continue to the room I woke up in, still flabbergasted that this is happening. I feel like I'm doing research for my next role. Maybe that's what this is. I'm just so wrapped up in the character I can't tell reality from my own design. But that can't be it. I'm losing my mind and I haven't even been up for more than a few hours.

In just over a week I'm supposed to be shooting a sequel called "The Beckoning Returns". If I can figure out what is going on before the start date, maybe everything will continue as planned. No, it won't be the case. Shit, what am I going to do? Walk on set and be like "Psyche!"

The first film, "The Beckoning" was about a group of friends going to a cabin and being killed off one by one by a masked serial killer. "The Beckoning Returns" is more or less the same premise, but this time the ones who survived are going back for revenge at a ski lodge. I haven't finished reading the script yet, but I know that this was going to be my last movie for a little while. I need a break. A big one that will leave me wanting to get back to work, not dreading getting on set and into character every few months.

I audibly groan as I sit on the bed and look around the room. I was still a bit groggy this morning to realize it, but there's a feminine touch to this room. Hand-made doilies rest on the bedside table—the newspaper isn't there anymore—the empty floral photo frames are clearer than this morning, and there are dried roses on the mantel with cobwebs twisted around the baby's breath. That's when I see it, a photo of Silas and his family sitting on the little hutch with too many drawers at the end of the bed. I distinctly remember this photo not being there this morning. Groggy or not, this photo wasn't there. Did Silas place this here? Why did he place this here?

I rise to peek at it, beautiful smiles glare back at me. He surely looks different without a beard, more distinguished and happier. The woman in the photo has dark hair like he does, and striking green eyes. They're brighter than his. Their son, however, isn't gifted with those light eyes. They're hazel, like mine. He also looks just like his father. It's funny how that works. My brother looks just like our dad, too. Whereas I resemble a bit of both my parents.

I always wondered what my kids would look like, but Adrien got a vasectomy before we met and refuses to reverse it. I can't blame him, either. Our hectic and chaotic life doesn't have time for children. I would be lying if I said the idea has not crossed my mind lately. My twenty-seventh birthday is in a couple of days. The closer I'm getting to thirty, the more I'm realizing maybe it's time to put my acting on pause and truly start that family I always wanted. I've accomplished a lot before my thirties, and it scares me to think once I hit that big 3-0, my chance of starting my family is riskier. Guess that dream's on pause now. At least until I know the truth.

I pick up the photo and study it some more. This wasn't taken at this house, it was at a park, I'm assuming a park back in the city. Silas' son's face is covered in blue and red frosting. He's very little in the photo, making me wonder how old he was when the car accident happened. The dark part of my brain wants to know all about it but it's not my place. I've never lost anyone before, never felt that grief people go through. The denial, the depression. My grandparents passed when I was very young, one of them still alive and living in a home.

The only loss I felt was my parents disowning me for my life choices. I again, cannot blame them. They are highly religious, and my choice of work—the films I play in especially—is against their beliefs. When I ran away, I was forgotten. My brother, even though not religious in the slightest, still hasn't spoken to me in ten years. More specifically, it'll be ten years to the day in two weeks.

My thumb grazes the photo, moving some dust out of the way. The happiness this photo blooms is unlike anything I can explain. Why do I need to know what happened to his kid? Am I that fucked in the head? No, I'm not. It's my morbid curiosity to learn about different emotions and experience new things for future roles.

I need a drink, and I need it badly.

I slip into the jeans I chose, realizing underwear should've been on that list, too, and grab the Harvard sweater. I like it. I've always liked wearing big clothing, especially Adrien's. He isn't fond of me wearing his t-shirts because I always stretched out the bust area. I never had the heart to tell him they're this big because of him. Three months after we got together, he offered to pay for implants to help speed along my career. I'd like to say that I regret them, but I don't. I barely had anything before. They make me feel attractive—and yes, they've helped me get roles because of sex scenes and whatnot. But I don't care. I love it when people stare at me.

I pull the sweater over my head and quickly apply some mascara before I make my way out of the room—sliding the knife into the sweater pocket. The floor creaks beneath my feet, sending that eerie chill the house already exudes. There's a looming presence in here, a presence I can't explain. Maybe it's the lingering loss of the little boy or the wonderment about what happened to his wife.

I hear grunts and strains, followed by cracks and slams. I make my way down the stairs to hear Marlow barking at the door from the outside; her nails scratch the metal frame. And see Silas through the glass windows in a wool sweater and that dark blue toque he hasn't taken off yet, chopping some firewood with a pipe in his mouth. It is much colder in the house than it had been this morning.

There is a charm to the house I admire. People pay to experience the cabin feel. Shit, Adrien wanted to invest in a lodge not far from here for that very reason. But it would never have the authenticity this house has. You can't fake something like this. The kitchen-dining-living room are all completely open. There's the counter and wall of shelves that separate the kitchen from the living room. I can still see into the living room through the shelves, but dishware blocks most of its view. It's warm and inviting. Cluttered with loads of knickknacks. But it feels like home.

After a while, I realize I'm watching Silas for way too long. Every time he swings the ax over his head he grunts, and brings it down on the log as if he's in pain. The thought that he was the cause of the car accident crosses my mind. That guilt riding through him, eating at him, and dissecting his thoughts. Could that be why he's alone?

He stops and looks up at Marlow, about to give her crap for barking like a lunatic when he catches my eye. I quickly look away, painstakingly obvious that I've been staring at him, and hear him let out a whistle to Marlow. Her barks die out immediately and I slowly sit at the table in the spot Silas was sitting in this morning. God, Parker. Make it more obvious that you were looking at him by sitting at the table with the perfect view.

It's weird, that shower helped relax my excited mind. I'm still freaked the fuck out. But there's a calmness washing over me. That dread that crawled along my skin from the moment I woke up, has subsided and my stomach is at ease.

The door opens moments later and Silas walks in with a boyish grin. Marlow charges in behind him and circles her bed twice before lying down. Silas places his pipe on a shelf by the door and tosses firewood into the fireplace on the other side of the house. I can kind of see him from where I'm sitting—the shelves blocking most of the view—a nasal grunt escapes him again before his heavy footfalls come my way.

"Um, do you need help with anything?" I ask, that uncomfortableness coming in as an awkwardness starts to encircle it. Yep, there's the churning in my stomach again.

"No." He looks at the sweater I'm wearing. "I take it you like the sweater?"

I rise and pull an arm out of the sleeve. "I can give it back—"

"No, no. Keep it," he interrupts. "I was wondering where that went."

I fix my sleeve, slowly sitting back down. 'So you really don't have a phone out here? No wifi? Nothing?"

"Nothing. I like it that way."

Well, I sure as hell don't. My heart leaps into my throat knowing even if I want to call for help, I can't. There isn't anything I can do but trust this man enough to help me.

"Then I insist, let me help with whatever you're doing." I was obsessed with my phone and obsessed with my Netflix account, maybe this silence and lack of paparazzi can be looked at as a good thing. A break. A much-needed break.

"You can keep sitting there and watching me," he teases, chuckling softly, and steps back outside. This man is a mystery and I want to know so much about him. I just can't understand why.

Chapter 5

Silas makes us lunch while I make us coffee. His cheeks are rosy from the cold, and he keeps rubbing his hands together. I can offer to make the sandwiches for him, but I don't. Being so close to him is intimidating. I keep the knife firmly in hand, but he doesn't try to lunge for it or stand too close to me to make me feel uncomfortable. He only points at things he needs when I'm in the way. My hands shake slightly as I make coffee, and my heart still thumps quickly. Being in his presence is both alluring and scary.

He puts on a record to fill the silence before he sits down. Country music to match his little accent that pokes through heavily when he isn't noticing. One thing I hate most when getting roles is having to play a part with an accent. Then again, I've nailed a British accent with the help of a coach. Australian I've tackled, but Texan. Ugh, I sound like an imp when I try to do that.

I wonder if it's where he's from, Texas. Or maybe Atlanta. It's safe to assume he went to Harvard, isn't it? I'm not obsessed, I swear. I just have to know everything about him in case, y'know, I was right and he is a crazy fan who wants to wear my skin as a suit.

"This sweater, it's yours?" I break the silence. So much so that Marlow looks up at me as if I disturbed her.

He takes a bite of his sandwich. "Mm, you're looking at a graduate."

"What'd you study?" I ask, having met my fair share of Harvard graduates.

He grunts, shifting in his seat. "Law."

"Work on any big cases I would know?"

It bothers me that he's practically a mute. Adrien doesn't mind how much I speak, well whatever he listens to at least. I'm not a fan of silence. Even alone, music always plays loudly, or some shows will be watching themselves in the background. It's probably why I love staying in New York City; there's always noise, always huddle, and always something to do.

"No," he answers and rises, tossing the rest of his sandwich at Marlow. She catches it and swallows it in one bite.

I think I hit a nerve. "Oh."

"Finish up. I'll bring you to the water where I found you." He disappears to the washroom with the red door.

"Yeah, okay." But I doubt he heard me.

I understand where he's coming from. He wants to keep his life private, much like I do from the spotlight. When I first got to Hollywood, I was seventeen with a thousand dollars I stole from my parents' church, and no experience or even a clue about where to start. I had drive, though. So much drive. Auditions were hard to come by, yet when I'd find one, I'd do whatever it took to get it. I never did. But I met so many great actors who took me in and guided me. I heard about the Bailey family through a close friend. They were known to take new actors under their wing and make them huge. So when a year went by after I had first arrived in Hollywood and not a single Bailey came my way, I knew I wasn't going to make it. Lo and behold, faith came knocking at my door that rainy day with nothing but a sexy smile and an umbrella.

I place my dish in the sink and look for a sponge to wash some of the dishes Silas joins me in the kitchen. "Don't bother, I'll do it later." He takes the plate from my hand and places it in the old bacon grease pan making me tense up and move away from him.

I take a breath, trying to get back to the state I was in before he stood so close to me. "You're not gonna let me do anything around here, are you?" He makes me nervous and excited and I can't fucking stand it.

"You're my guest—"

"I wouldn't call me a guest," I interrupt him.

"Well, I wouldn't call you my patient," he jokes, trying to ease some of the tension.

My lip quirks up but leaves just as quickly. "Guess that's fair."

His eyes lock on mine again, a long and lingering stare that irks the pit of my stomach with fear and intrigue. I'm not on the verge of puking anymore, which is a good sign I think. But I'm still on the verge of tears when I look out the window and realize I'm not home anymore. That my husband might have something to do with why people believe me to be dead. And why I can't remember anything about that night.

Silas' gaze softens and a grin touches his lips before he breaks our stare. Fifteen, maybe twenty seconds must've gone by before either of us moved. The most intense seconds of my life. I don't know him, yet all I want to do is stand there staring at him. He's a mystery and I can't help but want to drown in his aura of kind darkness.

"Ready to go for a walk, girl?" he says, scratching Marlow's ears. She barks and goes for the door, her nails scraping the floor. She's been outside almost all morning, but I think his presence makes her happy.

He hands me his jacket again, the tobacco wafts around me. "Is it far from here?" I ask, sitting on the bench by the door to put my boots on.

"Not too far." He stares at my bare feet as I slip them into the boots. "Want some socks?"

"Oh, um, if you don't mind."

He nods, disappearing again only to return with a folded pair of black socks in the shape of a ball. Silence spreads between us again as I finish getting bundled up and follow him into the cold.

Why did I think coming to Alaska was a good idea for my birthday? I already miss those warm days and walks in the sand. I love living in California. I love the crazed streets, the tourist areas, and the traffic. Everything about it makes me happy. I've always hated the snow, ever since I was a child. It depresses me and I'm not a depressed person. I'm full of life. But this gloomy place surely does a number to my happiness.

Silas sniffs, walking ahead of me and keeping his eyes on Marlow. It's rather pretty outside, aside from my nose feeling like it's about to fall off as it leaks every ten seconds. There are hundreds of birch trees spanning out with some pine trees that remind me of Christmas.

We had such a lovely Christmas this year. Adrien went above and beyond, getting decorators to make our home filled with Christmas cheer. We had three trees around the house. Our main one in the living room was ten feet tall with all the ornaments we collected over the years. A red and silver tree in the study, and my favorite gold with silver and white tassels in the entrance. The way it sparkled under the chandelier made it look like diamonds were hanging from it.

Adrien always gives me handmade gifts for anniversaries, birthdays, and Christmas. This year, however, I opened my present on Christmas morning to find a white gold necklace loaded with emeralds. It was so unlike him. Even my engagement ring isn't this flashy. I wish I noticed the signs, his differences. I wish I knew what the heck was going on.

Silas, Marlow, and I start descending the small slope that leads to a clearing, and water gurgles nearby. Marlow barks again and starts drinking some of the water, looking off at the vast nothingness around her. I let out a shuddered breath, trying to understand what happened to me. There's nothing here. Nothing! Just a dense forest that's kind of frightening and intimidating. How did I end up here?

"This is our fishing spot. I was checking on my lines when I saw you on shore," Silas says, looking at me.

I know the answer, but I ask anyway. "There was nothing on me?"

"Nothing." He keeps his gaze on the ground beside me. Why do I keep questioning it? Maybe it's because I want him to tell me that I'm dreaming. That this is a sick trick being played on me.

It isn't a trick, is it? This isn't my life.

How did my life come to this?

I look around and see nothing but tall dead grass, naked trees, and pine trees painted in snow. "What's out here?"

He points downstream. "There're a few houses that way. Not many folks like being by the river." He clears his throat as if hearing the why that went off in my head. "There's been flooding over the years because of the dam." He points in the other direction at a few hills of dirt. "Folks have been building up barricades by the river to avoid the floods."

I step closer to the water, Marlow at my feet, and look beyond the shoreline. Nothing looks familiar. The place Adrien rented isn't in this town or anywhere near the water. Silas said Anchorage is two hours away. So what the hell am I doing here? Ugh, I hate how foggy my brain is right now.

I strain my eyes downstream and see a dock. It's like a spec from this angle, but I'm assuming it's a dock, right? Could that be the dock I see myself dancing on?

"I can't remember a thing," I say softly. "All I see are flashes of things that don't make sense."

His breath clouds around us, dissipating in the air. "I found you right where Marlow's standing. I ain't going to lie, I had to give you mouth-to-mouth before you threw up water and bile. You weren't lucid, but you were alive." He nods. "Brought you home and forced you into a hot bath. You still didn't wake up, but you were alive."

"Why didn't you tell me this earlier?"

He sniffs. "You were in shock." He steps closer to me from behind. This is it. This is my time. It's my ending, isn't it? He didn't say anything because he wants to end me as he found me. I'm a liability now. Snap out of it, Parker. He's been nothing but helpful. "I thought bringing you here and telling you how I found you might spark your memories."

My head feels heavy like there's pressure. I'm not in my right mind, it's a given. I should be pressing him for answers. Digging as deep as I can. But I can't. I should call the cops, I should tell my story. Yet the dark side of Adrien's business is stopping me from thinking rationally. This is my break. This nightmare is a break from the reality of the situation that is my life.

I keep my focus on the rippling water. Thinking Silas might be right. A memory might spark. But it doesn't. "Do you think my husband killed me?"

"I don't know. But from what I read, it seems like he faked your death with a double and mangled up her face a bit so no one would know the difference."

Thank God I didn't read the magazine. This is too much.

Mangled?

Faked my death?

I can't take this agony.

I try to mask my sobs by placing a hand on my mouth, but it escapes. "Fuck."

I wish I had internet. I'd be able to contact someone, any-one. No one will believe me, how do I get these people to believe that I didn't die? Why would Adrien fake my death?

My shoulders are hunched and shaking, my mind is running around like a spinning top. I'm not ready for this. Who in their right mind can be ready for something as psychotic as this? I need answers. How in the hell am I supposed to get these answers?

A hand touches my shoulder and squeezes. I jump out of my skin, tensing again. I see his hands around my neck, squeezing, choking, killing. But he doesn't do anything. He leaves his hand on my shoulder until my sobs subside. I don't move. I don't turn around. I keep my focus on the water that could have killed me.

When I gaze at the dock in the distance, I see Adrien taking pictures of me as my toes touch the frozen wood. My hands are up in the air and I spin, letting the dress puff up around me. I remember laughing. Kissing. Smiling. Other than that, it's nothing but darkness.

Silas removes his hand. "You remember anything?"

I shake my head, lowering my shoulders. "Glimpses."

"Anything familiar?"

I wipe my cheeks and point. "The dock."

"The Kroger's?

I whip my head around and frown. "You know the house?"

He shakes his head. "No." Clears his throat and scratches the back of his neck. "Place is abandoned." Marlow barks and he snaps, shushing her. "No one's lived there in four years."

Well, if I wasn't freaked out before.

I'm staring at the dock, tempted to get in the water and see what's on the other side. But I fear one of Adrien's goons might be waiting there or scoping out the place in search of me. Who knew calling my husband would put me at greater risk than I was when I was naked in a river in the middle of winter?

"If no one's lived there in four years, explain why I see myself dancing in the living room. Or kissing my husband in the bedroom? And standing on the dock barefoot and—" I cover my face again, crying softly. "God, I need to call the police."

"You can't." He doesn't skip a beat. "It's not safe, especially if your husband knows you're alive." He shakes his head. "You shouldn't leave the house anymore—"

"I need to get on the internet."

"If people know you're alive, they might come back and try to kill you, Parker."

I scoff, roughly wiping my cheek. "You can't hold me captive."

"I'm not trying to."

"I'm getting on the internet."

He clenches his fists at his side, a slight twitch in his jaw, and wipes down his face. "It'll be dark soon. We should head back before it does."

"What?"

"It gets dark around three here."

I stomp my foot. "We aren't finished."

He gazes at me and walks away. Leaving a cloud of unfinished conflict between us.

I want to leave anyway. I feel everything closing in on me and I'm out in the open with nothing but forestry for miles.

I keep thinking that maybe Adrien's still here, just lurking in the shadows. There are things about Adrien I don't know. Parts of his business he keeps hidden. He is the son of a major producer, what more do I need to know? He's rich, famous, sexy as hell, and together we're dynamite. He checks all my boxes and has for eight years. Yet right now, my husband is as mysterious as Silas.

My sniffs move through the forest. I can't stop crying, but Silas doesn't seem to take notice. And that's okay, I rather he doesn't see me cry. I may be beautiful, but shit, I m an ugly crier.

Chapter 6

For the rest of the day, I lounge on the couch, reading a couple of chapters of some book he left on the coffee table. Carrie by Stephen King. I've heard of it but never gave it the time of day.

Silas has been outside most of the day, working in the shed, chopping more wood, and tending to Marlow. The silence isn't good for me, all I do is let my mind wander. It wanders into the houses Adrien and I live in, into our bedrooms, and our careers. The life we built is now ruined. Darkness clouds our life. I hate it, but I don't know how to fix it. I keep seeing different women we've met with Parisian accents. Brunettes, blondes, fuck, even a redhead rushes through my thoughts. Who is she? Why is she with Adrien?

"Hey," Silas says, startling me as I gaze into the fire in the living room.

I blink rapidly, turning to him. "Hi."

He raises his eyebrows, wiping his nose. "You said you wanted to help, yeah?" I nod, putting the book down. "Get dressed I need your help outside."

I wait for Silas by the front door as he goes to the washroom and watch Marlow let out a few barks outside. I'm not a handywoman by any means, so whatever he has planned for me better not mess up my freshly manicured nails. I love getting my nails done. Every holiday is expressed in the designs I choose. For New Year's, I chose a champagne color with my ring fingers painted sparkling gold.

Silas steps out of the washroom and flashes me a grin as he does up his pants. I don't even know him but I'm so fucking attracted to him. I see myself getting on my knees and pleasing him for everything he's done for me, hearing his moans move through the silence—I feel like a psycho for even thinking these dirty thoughts. You're married, Parker! You don't know what's going on yet, don't give up on Adrien that easily. But he tried to kill you. Move on and make this cabin a memorable one—look I'm talking to myself. I'm already losing it.

Silas steps outside, fixing the toque on his head before he picks up the ax from the tree stump. I stop, thinking the worst. He's going to chop my fucking head off, isn't he?

I rub my hands together. "What do you need help with?"

"Ever chop wood?" He takes his toque off and hesitantly hands it to me. Such a kind gesture, I'm kind of taken aback. His hair is kind of messy, but a just-had-sex kind of messy—and here I go again, mind in the gutter.

"No," I reply, putting the dark blue toque on. It's knitted and soft as hell. He wouldn't kill me. Not with his toque on. Of course, he wouldn't. He saved your fucking life already. Get it together, Parker.

He hands me the ax. "Here. It's easy."

I'm holding an ax, taken aback at the thoughts he might double-cross me. It's not what I expected and it's clear he isn't the man I thought he was. He's not my captor or my attempted killer. He's my savior.

He places a log onto the tree stump and looks at me as if I know what I'm supposed to do. It's a log on a tree stump. My aim is not the greatest. I will miss this log.

"I just swing and hit?"

"Just swing and hit," he repeats and smirks. "There's nothing to it...just loads of practice."

A small chuckle leaves me. "You're not going to hold it in place, are you?"

"Not if I wanna keep all my limbs." He eyes me again, his smirk growing into a smile. "I like my hands."

I lick my lips and squeeze my eyes shut imagining this log to be Adrien and that Parisian bitch on the phone. I swing and strike the log. The ax is stuck but Silas helps me pull it out and nods at the log for me to do it again. This time, I keep my eyes open.

"Ooh, this is a lot of fun," I say, finally breaking the log in half.

He points at the pile all over the ground. "Good, because we have that entire pile to get through."

I scrunch my nose. "Ugh, well, it's not that fun."

He lets out a laugh and nods. "All right, then. C'mon. I'll show you how to bar the windows."

"Bar the windows?"

"We got bears 'round here. Some of them are awake, some are still hibernating. There's wolves in these woods, too. Can't be too careful." He lifts one of the plywood boards, nodding at me to take the other. "Look, it's easy. Just place the plywood on the hooks and be careful of the nails sticking out."

I place the plywood on the hooks and wipe my hands on my jeans. "Has a bear ever broken in?"

"Not in the six years I've lived here." He grunts, lifting another piece of plywood. "I have seen my fair share roaming the woods."

"That's not scary," I say through a breath. Bears? I don't think I've ever seen a bear in real life. Not even at a zoo. I can't imagine coming across one near or on my property.

He helps me board up every window as the sun starts to set. He wasn't lying when he said it gets dark here early. Shit, and it's going to get really dark, really fast, too. I hate the dark. Every time I acted up as a child I'd get thrown into my room in utter darkness and told the devil will come knocking at my door if I kept it up. That stayed with me. I always sleep with a light on. Adrien never minded sleeping with a nightlight, either. He thought it was a cute quirk. I'm kind of happy there's a fire crackling in my room. I'll always have a light source.

Silas groans, taking the plywood from me and fixing it in place. "You're doing it wrong."

I screwed up twice, putting one of the plywood boards backward and skipping a window I can't reach. "I don't really know what I'm doing, now do I?"

A growl rumbles through him and his jaw tightens. Ooh, I struck a nerve. "Just go inside. I'll finish this."

I put my hands up in defeat and let them drop at my sides. "And do what? Sit on my ass staring at the four walls trying to figure out how the fuck I ended up in this godforsaken place?"

He scoffs, hooking the board on the window the right way. "Better than you doing this wrong. Miss a window and we can have a real problem on our hands."

I pinch the bridge of my nose, feeling a shiver run through me. "I didn't want this."

I.

Hate.

This.

Fucking.

Weather.

No, this place.

"You think I did?" He wipes his nose, sniffling. "You wanted to help. Sorry I don't have people to do things for me, Parker. Out here, we don't hire people. We man up and do the dirty work ourselves."

I scoff, shaking my head and adjusting his toque. "That was an asshole thing to say to someone who literally almost died." And out of her element.

Adrien does hire people to do the yard work and lean the house, but I wash my dishes and do my laundry. We have the means, might as well use it. "I hate this fucking place."

I go to walk away when Marlow brushes up against my leg and drops the ball at my feet. Great, now the dog wants me to do something I don't want to do.

Silas steps forward and takes the ball, throwing it to the back of the house, a grunt leaving him as he does. I sniff, hating this cold weather, but he doesn't seem to mind it. He's in nothing but a wool sweater, and rolled up his sleeves somewhere between the back of the house and the other side of the house.

"You're more than welcome to leave."

I grit my teeth and turn back to him. "And where in the fuck am I supposed to go?"

He shrugs and lifts another plank of wood with nails. "Ain't my problem."

"Of all people to save my life, I get stuck with someone like you." I scoff. "I thought you were sympathetic."

He laughs, mockingly. "You're welcome."

I growl and strut off, stopping when I realize how dark it is and how scary the surrounding forest looks at night. The tall trees remind me of shadows, looming over me. "Silas." I let out a breath. "I'm not as materialistic as you think I am."

He strains. "I don't care." And places the board on the last window of his house. "Your life back home is none of my business."

"Then why did you offer me to stay?"

He wipes his nose on the back of his hand again. "We come from two different lives. Yours is dramatic, mine is not. I offered you my home so you wouldn't be recognized in town."

"I'll leave in the morning."

"And go where?"

"Doesn't fucking matter, does it?"

I let my anger take over for a minute. I'm angry at this whole situation. I should be home with Adrien and eating leftovers from the New Year's Eve party. We should be making love all over our home, packing our suitcases, and drinking champagne for my upcoming birthday. I shouldn't be freezing my tits with a man I don't know, doing things I've never done, and crying every time I open my mouth.

Silas takes notice of my tears and lets out a breath. "You thirsty?"

"No." I shiver. "I'm freezing,"

"All right, let's get you inside. I should have enough wood cut for the night," he says, walking past me. I follow closely until the light from the front of the house illuminates the ground.

He escapes into the house as Marlow barks and charges for him, her feet skidding on the wooden floors.

I take a gander around before I follow because even though the dark scares me, it's intriguing. It's eerily quiet. There's nothing in the brush, but it feels like something is lurking in the darkness. The trees stand tall, naked, and alone. The pine trees seemingly sway from side to side as the wind brushes through the emptiness. Its howl creeps up on me and entraps me in its sound. I see figures, large and thin staring back at me. Observing me. My attempted killer is out there, waiting to finish what he started. I can feel their hands grabbing me as the breeze touches my face, pulling me into the dense abyss with them to be lost forever.

I yelp, feeling Silas' hand touch my shoulder. I was in such a trance as I stared out into the vast nothingness, I didn't hear Silas calling my name, nor did I hear his footfalls making their way toward me. All I hear is quiet.

He raises his eyebrows, hand still on my shoulder. "You all right?"

"Yeah, yeah. I'm fine."

He looks off at wherever I'm staring. "You see something?"

"No, no. It's just—it's so quiet here."

"You'll get used to it." He hesitantly places a hand on my lower back, but I shove his hand away. "Sorry." He looks off at the forest once more before heading inside.

Marlow barks at me and sits by her water bowl. Instinctually, I kick off my boots and fill the bowl. I don't think Silas wants me to do this because he takes the bowl from me. I don't really care. It is his dog after all. And in his eyes, I'm a snooty little rich bitch who has things done for her because I'm too much of a princess to do it myself. Dick.

"Do you have tea?" I ask, looking at the shelves in the kitchen.

His house doesn't have upper cabinets, only those open shelves I'm assuming he built out of a fallen tree. There's an array of cereal boxes, crackers, chips, condiments, loads of peanut butter, and coffee, but no tea. Mm, he has Oreo cookies.

He looks over his shoulder. "I don't drink tea. I got decaf coffee if you're worried you won't sleep tonight."

"No, no. Regular coffee is fine." I look around again. "You ever get lonely out here?"

He grunts, shaking his head, and starts fixing the coffee maker. How could someone live alone without anyone for six goddamn years? If I'm left alone for six hours, I'll lose my mind. I'm a people person and I love being around loved ones—well, the ones who actually give a shit which is very few. Adrien is the one I spend ninety percent of my time with, and most of that time, we're moaning instead of talking. I'm not going to complain about that. I love it. But it's nice to have that partner to be yourself around. What's your story, Silas? You've pissed me off but you've also intrigued me.

Silas stays quiet as he prepares us coffee, the scratching of vinyl is still spinning on the record player. Adrien produces films, but every now and again, he'll produce a music artist. We have a small vinyl collection in the study that we listen to on those nights we get drunk together. Adrien loves dancing with me. Even when there isn't any music playing, he'll take my hands and hold me close to him as we sway. I hope I'm wrong and he didn't try to kill me. I can't lose the only person I love most in this world. What am I going to do without him? God, what the actual fuck is going on?

Silas places a cup of steaming coffee in front of me. "Just sugar, right?"

I keep staring into space. Maybe I should go see a doctor? No, no. I'll be fine. The fewer people I see the better until I speak to someone who will help me. Right? Cops. Tomorrow I'll call the cops. I'll speak with someone who isn't in Adrien's pocket. What are the odds of that happening? Shit. I should have called the cops this morning. Why am I such an idiot?

"One sugar." I hold the mug in my hands and inhale its goodness. "So what do you do for fun around here?"

"There ain't much to do if you haven't noticed."

"I have." I lick my lips which are starting to get chapped. "Running from the law or something?"

"No." He laughs with me, sitting beside me at the table. I don't know why, but the head of the table is my go-to spot. "Don't gotta big family."

"Yeah, me neither." Although I have no idea what my brother is doing with his life right now, nor my parents.

"I have loads of books over there, and there's a TV in my room if you ever wanna watch a movie or something. Have a small collection by the fireplace." He points at the bookshelf by the stairs and the little shelf of DVDs by the fireplace, which is roaring with flames.

I bite my lower lip and raise my eyebrows. "Oh, I wouldn't want to impose."

"I don't mind moving it." He puts his leg out as Marlow places her head on it. He scratches behind her ear, then looks at me. "She's taking a liking to you. She doesn't warm up to people this easily. She still hates the vet and he's the only one in town."

I chuckle and look down at Marlow. "I'm easily likable."

She lifts her head and opens her mouth as if she's smiling. She's cute, I'll give her that.

I sigh, looking at the dark liquid in front of me. "Has anyone come looking for me?"

He shakes his head. "News broke in town that you were found at the Kroger's. That's it."

I scoff. Some fucking family I have. "No cops came by? Reporters? Nothing?"

He shakes his head.

I know the answer already, but I ask anyway. "Did Adrien come by?"

"No one came by, Parker." He taps the table. "This is a small town. Murders aren't something that happens here often."

"You figure fame would change that."

"Fame changes nothing."

Ouff, that hit hard. But he's right. Fame changes nothing when you need help. My close friends and family haven't flown out to see if the tabloids are real. I guess it's true what they say, people believe anything they read.

There I go again. My eyes well with tears and they slowly fall, skimming my cheeks.

He's staring at me and hasn't stopped since we started speaking. I should feel intimidated. Scared. But I'm not. I guess seeing where I almost died changed something. There's this trust I'm letting build because I have no one else.

"Was gonna make chicken, you okay with that?"

I don't know him, but if he stares at me like this any longer, I might either have to smack his face or rip his clothes off. It could go either way at this point. God, I'm one twisted fuck. "Whatever's fine."

The darkness pools in by the window above the sink. It doesn't even look real from where I'm sitting. It's like I'm staring at a black painted canvas hanging just above the sink where he's rinsing the full chickens. Wait, who the hell rinses chickens?

Marlow starts barking manically at the front door. Her barks turn to growls, then snarls, and the hair on her back lifts. Silas sighs and looks over at her, a disgruntled look about him. She must do this often because she hears something outside. I don't blame her, I want to scream, too, just to fill in the silence that's making my ears ring. "Enough," he raises his voice.

I gulp my coffee. "She okay?"

"Yeah, probably hears some animal outside."

I nod and look at the door again. The large windows to either side of it are boarded up. I'm assuming this is something he does every night and removes every morning I wonder if a bear has ever come up to the house. I think I'd shit myself if I saw it. I'm scared of my own reflection for Christ's sake, I could only imagine what a bear would do to me. Faint? Yeah, most probably.

"Do you need any help?" I ask, feeling a little out of place just sitting here watching him. I can only watch him for so long before it becomes creepy.

I don't cook much at home, I prefer baking. During the week we order most of our meals and cook on weekends. Although my favorite is our anniversary. We make sure to use our kitchen to its fullest potential and cook a feast—naked, of course.

Silas smirks, shutting the tap. "You peel potatoes before?"

I widen my eyes. "Yes."

A laugh leaves him, it's deep and contagious. I don't take offense to what he asks. I'm not like most celebrities. Every Christmas we have a huge feast with our closest friends and

Adrien's family. His father, Colm, was never my biggest fan. He thought Adrien should have made me a somebody, then left me, and moved on to the next. Instead, Adrien made me more than somebody, fucked me silly, married me, and continued to fuck me silly while helping other new actors and actresses make names for themselves. I'd put money on my death being Colm's fault. Mind you, Adrien never does anything his father asks of him. He likes doing things his way and his way always gets him paid. This is why he's fighting for the position of the owner of Bailey Industries once Colm passes.

Silas and I make dinner together. I peel the potatoes, and Silas roasts the chicken and fries up a few veggies. I clear my throat, watching the water boil, and glance at him. From the little conversations that we've had, I have to pry information out of him. There's something about him that makes me want to talk. I hate silence and he's friggen swimming in it.

"What's your all-time favorite meal?"

He regards my questions with a shrug, opening the oven to remove the tin foil from the chicken. He's not that easy to talk to but he sure can listen.

"I love me some shepherd's pie. My mom used to make hers differently. She'd add onions, peas, carrots, and turnips to the ground beef. Oh, and she'd leave the skin on the potatoes when she mashed them." I salivate at the memory. "I haven't had a meal like that in years."

He nods, wiping his hands on the dishcloth. "My sister makes a good rib rub. Best in Texas, if you ask me."

"You have a sister?" Now I feel like I'm getting somewhere. "Is it only the two of you?"

He stirs the veggies in the frying pan and adds some salt to it. There it is again. Silence.

"Do you still practice law?"

"No."

I tongue my cheek and stare at the little bubbles forming in the pot. "If I needed a lawyer for this bullshit, would you help me out?"

"I don't practice anymore, Parker."

I hate the way he says my name. "I guess you'd also be a conflict of interest, given that you're the one who saved my life." I nod, stirring the boiling potatoes. "I don't know who to trust anymore. Adrien is the one who dealt with all the legal crap. I wouldn't even know where to start if I got access to my money and found a way out of here."

"You don't have your own attorney?"

"Everything is in both our names." I shrug. "We have a shared bank account."

Silas lets out a rush of air, poking at the veggies as if he's coming up with a way to help me. He is a lawyer after all. There's got to be something he learned in all the years he practiced that can be of some use.

Silence.

Again.

Six minutes go by before I open my mouth. "You like the quiet."

"That's why I live out here."

I nod, poking a potato with a fork. "I'm a city girl, silence is deadly. I love noise." I lift the pot to the sink and strain the potatoes. "We were planning on moving to New York this year. Selling one of the houses and buying something in Central Park."

He watches me over his shoulder. "Never been."

"It's something else."

I start mashing the potatoes as Silas puts on a record of Johnny Cash. I don't mind it so much, Adrien fancies him, too. But as soon as the music starts playing, the conversation between us is silenced almost completely. We're the complete opposite and I'm starting to dislike this arrangement. I just want to go home, but I fear there's nothing left to go home to.

I study Silas a lot, staring at his mannerisms, and his movements. When he blinks, they're always in twos. He scratches his chin at least six times every couple of minutes. And my favorite is how he avoids staring at me, even though I catch his lingering eyes. He has this caring aura about him, too. It's that fatherly instinct. I'm sure once upon a time he was a brilliant lawyer. Everything is thought over, and precise, and there isn't a line for error. He holds himself well, but there's a fog around him he's suffocating in. Losing a child will do that. Yet he's calm. Always so calm. I admire this, I admire a lot about him, I just wish I knew more.

Chapter 7

My mind doesn't shut off, even after dinner and after Silas and I say good night. I can't sleep because all I think about is having a drink. At home when I couldn't sleep, I'd escape to the study and curl up on my favorite armchair with a glass of whatever I could find.

As fear claws at my inside, I slip out of bed and grip the doorknob. I don't turn it. Not yet. It's dark as hell outside. There isn't a light in my room aside from the lamp on the side table and the glow of the fire. I don't know what to expect on the other side of this door. So I peek out, just enough for my imagination to run wild. This tall looming creature builds in the shadows of the hallway. Its many long, unnatural arms stretch out to me, I swear I hear it howling my name. No, that's just the wind outside, Parker. It's the wind.

I close the door anyway, a soft whimper escaping me. I don't need a drink. I don't need a drink. I don't need a drink—fuck, I need a drink.

My shaking hands try this again. The hair on the back of my neck rises, goosebumps have spread from my head to my toes, and there's this tingle of fear and uneasiness in my stomach. I'm going to puke if that thing is out there.

I creep out of the room, there is nothing here.

Every step I take is slow and thought out.

The fire crackles in the living room and I make my way over, knowing I saw bottles on the mantle. Or was it beside it? Either way, there's booze in the living room.

I'm in nothing but the giant Harvard sweater, thinking Silas is asleep and I can get away with being pretty much naked in his house. I love being naked, but I'm starting to realize that this isn't my house and it's dark out here and I'm already on edge. I don't like this.

I'll grab a bottle and get back to my room. In and out.

The wind howls once more, and I shoot my attention to the front door. It's boarded up yet all I can see is someone standing behind it. Taunting me. Tapping their fingers so delicately on the door, it's enough to emit another whimper from me. I'm living a nightmare.

I tiptoe into the living room and jump as Silas clears his throat, a drink in one hand as the other is petting Marlow's head.

I put my hand to my chest. "Goddammit."

"Can't sleep?"

"No," I say, sitting in the armchair by the fire.

He takes a sip of his drink. "Mm."

It's only then I notice he's shirtless. He's a lot more muscular than I imagined. Cutting all that wood must be the reasoning. As I study his shirtless torso cast in the orange and yellow glow of the flames, I spot a deep scar across his abdomen that curls up his rib cage and disappears behind him. What a gnarly-looking gash. It's so intriguing, yet so disturbing. I can't look away.

He takes notice of me staring and clears his throat. "You have any scars?"

I switch my gaze to his eyes. "Hmm?"

His eyebrows raise. "Do you have any scars?"

"N-no." I don't really want to explain the scarring under my tits from the implants. "Sorry, I didn't mean to stare."

"It's okay." He gulps his drink. Judging from the bottle sitting on the coffee table in front of him, this isn't his first of the night.

"Can't sleep, either?"

"Hard to sleep out here sometimes."

"It's the maddening silence." I look at the ceiling as a creak moves through the house. This is what I hate about older homes, there's always something moving in it even though there's nothing there.

"Mm," he agrees, those piercing jade eyes shooting through me. "Still not used to the quiet."

I curl my legs up on the armchair. "Why do you say that?"

"Last few years I spent here have been the first time I was alone my whole life." He slurs a little and gives me another once-over. His gaze stays on my exposed legs for a moment too long. He's a little drunk. Maybe drunk Silas will open up to me? "It's funny, my ex-wife never used to wear my clothes." He says clothes with a lisp. "She was tiny and liked to keep her clothes tight. Especially when she was pregnant." He moans softly, petting Marlow's head. "Her favorite thing to do was dress up for parties or events and such, but never did she once wear something of mine."

I don't know what to say. He's opening up to me. Should I respond? Or just let him speak. I can't help it, I have to know about his life. It's like this irritable urge that needs to be fulfilled. An addict looking for a fix. A drunk needing a drink. Sobriety will meet her maker tonight.

"I don't mean to wear your sweater all the time," I say under my breath. "I don't have much else."

"It's no bother." He gives me a little grin. "I like it."

He likes it.

Silence spreads for a moment as he takes a sip. I want a drink so badly. I hope he has something other than whiskey.

I poke the bear until my sadistic mind knows everything about him. "Um, how long were you and your wife together?"

"Six years," he answers. "She was a paralegal at my firm. Six months after we met she got pregnant. We weren't in a relationship when it happened, either. Just fooled around a little. She always used to say that if it wasn't for Jack, we wouldn't be together. I don't want to believe it, but I know it's true. Funny how things turn out, ain't it?"

I look at the fire, blinking slowly. "Where is she now?"

"She left after Jack died. We didn't last more than three weeks before she left in the middle of the night without a note. She always said this place reminded her of Jack." He stirs the liquid in his glass. "Guess the silence was too much."

"What happened to your son?" I ask, seeing the words float out to him and clamp my lips shut. "Sorry, I shouldn't have asked."

He takes a sip. "Mm."

"I wanted Jack to see what snow was. We came down for a weekend and went for a walk in the forest. Little did I know it was hunting season." He points at his neck. "Bullet got him right in the jugular." He frowns, clearing his throat. "On the way out of here, I crashed into a tree when I heard Jack take his last breath." He shoots back the rest of his drink and lets out a sharp breath. "I got this scar from that." His hand slides over his stomach. "The last thing I heard before I passed out was her screams for Jackie."

I have my hand on my mouth, tears falling from my eyes. Why the fuck did I ask? I can only imagine what he must be going through, and what his wife is going through. I don't have kids, but that seems like it hurts so much more than losing someone close to you.

He rises, making Marlow growl softly, and get off the couch to her bed by the door. Silas pours himself another drink and takes a second glass, filling it up just as high as the one he places on the table.

I take the drink and gulp from it, feeling the sting rush down my throat. "I'm sorry," I whisper.

"Shit happens." He sighs. "Pure dumb luck."

"Have you spoken to your wife since she left?"

"No." He clears his throat. "Like she said. If it wasn't for Jackie, we wouldn't be together."

Silence brews once again, the crackling of fire taking over. I don't mind it this time. I feel like I need a breather after what he dropped on my lap. How can someone move on after that?

I have no words. For the first time in my life, I have absolutely nothing to say.

"Do you have kids?" he asks, breaking the awkward silence.

I shake my head. "I'd be lying if I said I don't want any, but Adrien had a vasectomy before we met and refuses to reverse it. So, no kids for me."

"He's a big-time producer, isn't he?"

"Yep, he doesn't want to take time off work if we have kids, either. Plus we wouldn't be able to up and leave on a whim when we feel like we need a break. Yeah...it's fine," I say, sipping my drink. But it's not. I want kids so badly.

He licks his lips, his eyes are small and narrow. He is very drunk right now. "Where you from?"

"Originally from Vermont. Ran away when I was seventeen and made my way to Hollywood." I look in the glass, remembering the guilt that rode through me the night I left.

"Why'd you run away?" he asks, now it's his turn to pry.

"My dad's the preacher of the town. They thought I was a devil worshiper when I stopped attending Sunday mass in favor of gossip magazines, romance novels, and boys. Well, one boy...they completely disowned me when I left," I pause and take a breath. "I don't blame them, I did steal a grand from the donations at the congregation to help me get to Hollywood."

"Ever pay 'em back?"

"I send them money all the time, but none of the checks are ever cashed."

He holds my gaze for a moment, his tongue teasing his bottom lip. "Have you ever gone back to visit?"

I shake my head quickly. There's no way in hell I'd ever set foot in that town again. I could only imagine what they said about me. What they think of me now and what they think of me in general. They probably used me as an example in their services about what not to do.

"Religion was a big thing in our house, stupid big. I had a cross above my bed and wasn't allowed to hang posters or listen to music that they didn't approve of. I was drowning if that makes sense. Movies were my escape. I'd sneak out of my room to catch the late viewings of movies they didn't approve of at the local theatre." A smile touches my lips as I sip the drink. "When I watched Breakfast At Tiffany's one night, I knew I wanted to be just like Audrey. I wanted people to see me on the big screen. When I told my mom, she threw holy water at me. I left two days later," I say, bringing my knees to my chest, making sure to hide the fact that I'm not wearing underwear.

"Mm," he grunts, getting comfortable on the couch. He scooches down so his head rests on the back of it and opens his legs wider.

The silence is back and I gulp down the rest of my drink, hoping it'll help me relax. It doesn't. I can't stop seeing the sadness and pain in his eyes when he talks about Jack. The son he lost over a stupid mistake. Tears well in my eyes again, reimagining what he told me. He lost his son. I can't even begin to know what to say to him anymore.

"My brother's name is Jack, too," I spit out, snapping my lips shut as soon as I do. "Sorry, I didn't mean to—"

"We named him after my father."

I hold up my empty glass. I need to steer away from the death talk. "You mind if I have another?"

He sits up and pours me another hefty glass, tilting his to me and downing the rest before he tops himself off. His eyes are glassy, which tells me he's probably been drinking a while now. I would too if I were in his shoes. A woman who doesn't love him stays with him because of their baby. Once their baby is gone, so is she. He lost everything and he still sits here with this selfless aura about him, helping me. We need more people like Silas in this world.

He stares at me with this glare like he wants to do something. "We'll try your family again tomorrow if you like?" His stare intensifies when his eyes shift to my legs.

"Is there a place I can use the internet?" I thumb my lip, a thought coming to mind. "If I up and call my family they'll think it's a joke after what the news is saying. But if I get ahold of someone and show them it's me, then I think I'll be able to get outta here and figure out what's happening."

He nods, staring into his drink like he's contemplating his next move. With another lick of his lips, he looks up at me. His stare is so intimidating, but I don't feel scared. There's kindness in there, generosity, and that selflessness I admire. He raises his glass to his lips and looks me up and down.

Goddamn, there's a rush going through me. Twisted up in knots in the most intimate place. How can someone who has lost so much have such intimidation about them? Sadness isn't on his face anymore. It's something else. And the sick part of my brain wants to test out what it can be.

But I won't. I'm a married woman. Married to a man who may or may not have tried to kill me.

Loyalty.

Devotion.

Fright.

Silas' stare is borderline frightful at this point. Everything he wants to say, he says with his eyes. This much I've learned. He isn't much of a talker, but those eyes tell every bit of his story. And right now, they're scaring the shit out of me.

I let out a shaky breath. "What?"

"Nothing."

"You're staring at me like you want to say something."

He shakes his head and sinks into the couch a bit more, flickering his gaze at the fire. "Does your husband dabble in more than producing?" He downs his drink and coughs softly.

"What do you mean?" I ask, knowing how dangerous Adrien's extra income can be when he isn't producing.

"I've represented a producer or two, and most aren't the cleanest of people if you know what I mean." He clears his throat. He's a lawyer, he knows more than I do about Adrien's business. "I've represented Hank Whitehall before his accusations of sexual harassment came out."

"Oh," I say, looking at him with the answer written all over my face.

"Mm." He looks away from me to the painting above the fireplace. It looks like a Jackson Pollock. The black background has blotches of white and splatters of red. I never understood art, that was Adrien's department. We'd gone to so many galleries and dropped thousands on paintings he said: "moved him". I don't get it, half the ones we own look like misshapen rectangles.

"I stay out of that side of his business."

He nods, getting comfortable on the couch again and glaring at me. That stare is going to get him into trouble.

We don't say anything else for the remainder of the night. We watch the fireplace and drink in silence. I'm not sure when, but I fall asleep in the armchair curled in a ball. I hear Silas grunt quietly when he gets up and places a blanket on me. Chivalry oozes out of him. I learned a lot tonight, and it makes me believe that maybe I was brought here for a reason. I'm still trying to figure out this reason, but maybe this is my second chance at life. Instead of faking my way for a paycheck, I can do something good. Maybe it's a break. I sure do need a break.

One thing's for sure, showing the world what a fucking dick my husband is. How he tried to do this to me for God knows what reason...but I love him, that's what's hurting me. Why would he try to kill me if he loves me, too?

CHAPTER 8

L oud rapping strikes the door, startling me awake. Silas snorts and opens one eye before Marlow starts yapping. I groan and stretch out my legs. The knocks sound again, causing Marlow to bark madly. Banging and straining are heard. Whoever is at the door is removing the boards on the large floor-to-ceiling windows. Jesus fuck, please don't let it be someone here to finish the job.

Silas whips the covers off me, peering behind him. It's a man in a uniform holding his hands around his eyes, looking through the window and into the house. It's a cop!

"Get on the couch and lie down," Silas instructs.

"What? Why?" This is what I want. I want someone to know I'm still alive.

He pulls his wool sweater from the back of the armchair and gets into it. "Billy ain't someone to trust."

I scoff, glancing at the front door. "And I'm just supposed to take your word for it?"

"Yes." He grits his teeth, standing above me and making me feel two feet tall. "He'll lead you right to your deathbed. That what you want?" He buttons up his sweater as Billy bangs on the window. "Get on the couch."

I do as he asks and creep onto the couch, pulling the covers on me, the warmth of his body still lingers under them. My lower lip quivers. I should be up and pleading with the cop to help me. I should make myself known and explain my situation. But Silas hasn't lied to me. Why would he lie about this?

Shit.

Get off the couch and make yourself known, Parker.

Get off the couch.

GET OFF—

Silas squints and unlocks the door, nodding at the cop. "Morning, Billy. What can I do you for?" His voice cracks, its deep rasp leading a shiver through me and shushing Marlow.

Billy takes something out of his breast pocket. "Don't know if you read about the actress that showed up dead in the waters out back on Canyon Road."

Silas slides his hands into his sweater pockets. "Saw some headlines when I picked up groceries yesterday."

Billy holds up a photo of me. "Her husband says someone is pranking him, or some such bullshit, and asked us to ask around again to see if anyone's seen her."

Why doesn't Silas just tell him the truth?

He jerks his head at the photo. "I know what Parker Bailey looks like. If she was pronounced dead, why's he asking you to ask around?"

"The fuck should I know?" Billy stuffs my photo back in his pocket. "Something about the coroner's report coming back and the body that they found wasn't Miss Bailey's."

Silas nods slowly, folding his arms across his broad chest. "Did you question her husband? See what he knows?"

I slowly lift my head, seeing their reflection in a mirror by the stairs. Billy is overweight and balding. He may not be someone to trust according to Silas, but he sure looks like he's done with his job. Even his uniform isn't pressed. His shirt is untucked, and his badge is in his hand rather than affixed to his shirt.

"He's been detained until yesterday. They did tests on him and part of his story checks out. His blood alcohol levels were off the charts, and he had ketamine in his system. They're trying to figure out what really happened here. FBI is scoping the area. If they come asking questions, tell them whatever you know." Billy nods. "Shit like this doesn't happen in Talkeetna."

FBI? Is this cop for real? What the actual fuck is going on here? I have to get ahold of my husband again and figure out what's happening.

Silas cocks an eyebrow, looking down at Marlow as she growls softly. "I ain't got nothing to tell."

Billy pushes his lips together, tapping his badge on his hand before stuffing it into his pocket. "Well, just holler if you see anything."

"Mm." Silas readies himself to close the door when Billy puts his foot out making slush fly off his boot and into the house.

"Who was that woman you were shopping with yesterday?" Billy inquires. "Mary said she saw you with someone."

I'm about to jump off the couch and speak up. But when Billy pulls out a pen and starts clicking it, I stop. It's a Bailey Industries pen. My husband's fucking pen. Silas was right. There truly is no one to trust.

Silas scratches his chin. "Just my girl visiting from out of town."

"Good to see you happy again," Billy says, which pains me to think of Silas sad.

Silas grunts. "Mm."

Billy looks over his shoulder into the house, scoping it without stepping foot inside. "I reckon you've heard? They're putting up a cell phone tower on this side of the river. Might be a good idea to get yourself a phone soon."

Marlow lets out another couple of barks before Silas shushes her, nudging her outside to do her business, then nods at Billy. "Yeah, I'll think about it."

"Have a good day now." Billy looks into the home once more and I watch through the reflection of the mirror as he retreats to his car.

Silas leaves the door slightly ajar and heads to the kitchen to start a pot of coffee. I let the words flow from my mouth before I even can think about what I'm saying. "You should've told him I was here," I say, getting off the couch and coming to the kitchen.

Marlow's barks are directed at me as she charges into the house. "Go lay down," Silas snaps.

"If they're looking for me, that means Adrien will stop at nothing to find me—"

Silas speaks through gritted teeth. "Billy ain't someone to trust."

"And you are?" I scoff, tears rolling down my cheeks. "I don't fucking know you! For all I know you're the one who tried to kill me in the first place."

"I took you in and helped you, didn't I? I could've left you for dead but I didn't." Silas raises his voice, snapping his fingers as Marlow tries to get off her dog bed.

"Then why won't you let me talk to the cops? There's got to be someone else who is trustworthy?" I snap, stomping my foot like a goddamn child. "You can't keep me locked up here!"

Silas opens the front door, a cold draft sweeping in. I can still hear the roar of Billy's engine moving down the path. "You wanna trust him, by all means. Go right ahead."

I start biting the inner part of my lip and look out the door. What am I doing? I have nowhere to go, no one to trust or talk to. But I'm aggravated because there should be something I can do instead of sitting here and expecting the answers to fall onto my lap.

I scoff and storm up the stairs to the washroom. I honestly feel like I'm stuck at a fork in the road. Up ahead is Adrien and all the lies and secrets he keeps hidden are brewing to the surface. To my right is Silas, his kind and well-natured manner to help me will not go unnoticed. And to my left are the cops. I don't know what to do because I don't even know who to trust.

CHAPTER 9

I don't have breakfast with him, nor do I leave the room he lets me sleep in. Instead, I cry. I cry because no one is trying to look for me aside from the person that I believe tried to kill me. No one cares that I'm gone. All those friends I thought I had were just friends for my status. Weren't they?

I cry because I feel so alone.

After I can't take the boredom of staring at the four dusty walls, I make my way out of the room in the jeans I wore yesterday and a black tank top I found in the closet. This is my weekend look back home. I love the simplicity of not caring if I'm wearing a brand name or not.

I spin my hair into a high ponytail and see Silas sitting at the head of the table, sanding a little side table he must've built. It looks like the side table in my room. I don't say anything and sit at the table, watching as he sands down the rough edges. His cheeks redden as id sensing my stare, but he keeps his focus on what he's doing. I know I shouldn't have snapped, I just couldn't help it. I'm pissed. I'm scared. I want to go home. But I don't even know if there's a home to go to. I'm alone, remember? I'm hoping someone hears my message and my family can find it in their hearts to forgive me. I need their forgiveness now more than ever.

"You hungry?" he breaks the silence.

"Um, yeah." I look out the window at Marlow sniffing at the ground. "Sorry for my outburst earlier."

"Did you notice the pen?"

I sniff, keeping my focus on Marlow. "I did."

He blows at the corner he's sanding. "He ain't someone to trust."

"What do you think it means?"

He shrugs, sanding softly at the other corner. "They got here before the FBI or whoever is investigating your death."

I put my head in my hands and shake it. "This is so fucked-up."

He finally looks up at me, taking my shuddered breathing and how I bite my quivering lip. The cold licks up my spine, making the reality of my situation hurt so much more. "We're gonna figure this out, Parker."

The facts. What are my facts?

1) I'm in Alaska in a town two hours from where I'm supposed to be.

2) I was drunk and probably drugged on New Year's Eve.

3) My husband is with some French bitch and presumably tried to kill me.

4) This sleepy little town's sheriff is affiliated with my husband.

Now, how do I play into all of this? It just doesn't make sense. Who did Adrien piss off enough to try and kill me?

Silas clears his throat. "Wanted to head into town again, see if you got any messages, then we'll head to the café to use one of the computers. You good with eating there for lunch?"

I laugh, sniffling. "Like a date?" Humor is my coping mechanism. He laughs with me, it's cute, making me feel bad for how I reacted earlier. It makes me think of Adrien. The love and admiration I thought we had for each other. He's my everything. I guess I'm not good enough to be his. "What do you think Adrien is up to with the cops?"

Silas blows softly at the corner of the table. "Tying up loose ends." He might be right. If Adrien believes I'm dead, why is he asking around? Can it be because he isn't involved?

NO! He's involved, Parker. Some French bitch answered the phone remember? He told you you'd never see the light of day.

He's bad news. It's apparent, but I can't say goodbye. Not yet.

"You're a carpenter?" I desperately need to change the subject I brought up. Just for a minute.

"My dad was. Taught me a thing or two." Silas smiles. "Built this very table you're sitting at two years after Jackie died. Needed a distraction, y'know."

I lean my elbow on the table and rest my chin on my hand. "Does your family come to visit you?"

"Not in the last couple of years. Mom died when I was a teenager, my sister still lives in Dallas with her girlfriend and their two kids, and my younger brother's at NYU." He nods, frowning slightly. "Dad floats around from Dallas to

New York, he doesn't come out here much. Not a fan of the snow."

Mm, touchy subject when it comes to his father. It's okay, I enjoy how he's getting a little more comfortable with me to open up. Maybe I'll help him open up a little more and he'll represent me if I need a lawyer for whatever bullshit is happening to me. "Understandable."

He scratches his nose with his forearm. "Mm."

I admire the way he sands and softly blows the dust away. I now understand why it's so dusty in here. I like to study people, it's a quirk my agent taught me to better understand people and their mannerisms. It's what got me an Oscar, too. And I like to study Silas. He fascinates me. A broken man who hides his pain through solitude and silence.

As my eyes roam over him, I notice he coiffed his beard. Did he tame the disaster it was because of me? Maybe he did, or maybe it was time to tidy up the straggling hair that looked matted on his face. He looks better now. A lot better.

Marlow starts barking at the door, scratching to come in. Instinctively, I get up and open it for her, making myself at home it seems. Her barks don't die down, clearly, not used to having people around. Silas grabs her by the collar and drags her to her bed, shushing her quietly.

"She always this rowdy?"

A smirk touches his lips and he looks up at me, tapping Marlow's side before disappearing to the washroom. There's this love toward her as if all his fatherly instincts went to raising and training her after his son passed. Seeing them on the couch last night brought such sadness to me. He must've done that with Jack a lot. Must've wanted to raise his son to be handy like he is. To flourish in the woods, and know simple survival tactics. But that will never happen. Silas is trapped here. Trapped with the guilt of his son's death.

"Ready when you are," Silas sounds, getting into his puffy vest.

I nod and slip my feet into my boots, readying myself to try and contact someone. I could call my best friend Alexis, but then again, I don't even know her number by heart. If I can get to a computer, maybe there's a webcam I can record a video on with today's new paper as proof that I'm alive and email it to her.

I don't know who the woman is that they chose to pretend to be me, but she must've been convincing for the authorities to pronounce me dead.

What is your motive, Adrien? Why would you do this to me? To us?! You killed some poor woman for what? My brain hurts when I try to think about what the reason could be. It's not for money, we have that. What is it?

*

The drive to town is silent. We leave Marlow at home so we can eat out without worrying about her in the car. Although, I'm still not sure how I'm supposed to dine out without being recognized.

That's the most annoying thing about being a celebrity. I never have a moment of peace. There's always someone watching. Always someone bothering. And want to know something even more annoying? It never stops. Not when I'm with Adrien having dinner or having coffee with Alexis. Not even when I'm doing groceries. I just want a fucking break from the life of a celebrity. And now, seeing my name on every tabloid, I'm even more exposed.

We drive past the corner store to a little quaint café with a sign that reads free Wi-Fi with the purchase of a coffee. He pulls in and clears his throat, fixing the toque on his head.

I take the sunglasses from the cup holders separating us. "Do they have the local paper here?"

"Yeah." He watches me slide them on. "Why?"

"I don't know. I had this idea that I'd record a video holding the local paper and send it to my best friend. She's the only one I can think of that would believe me because she's never been a fan of Adrien." I groan, leaning back in my seat. "It's stupid, isn't it?"

"No, it's a good tactic. Gotta start somewhere."

"Exactly." I sigh, putting a hand on my face. "Ugh, I'm so confused. I don't understand why he would do something like this."

"Neither do I," Silas says, giving me a quick grin. "Listen, you're welcome to stay as long as you need to, I don't mind. Least until all this is sorted."

I don't even think it over. I take this as my chance to breathe. As messed up as that sounds, I need a break. I'm overworked. Tired. The world thinks I'm dead. I have no idea why. My husband may have killed me. What's a couple of days in seclusion to figure it out and try to relax? "Thanks."

"All right, I'm going to head to Mary's and see if there was a call for you, then we'll eat?" He takes his toque off and puts it on my head. I flinch. But this trust for him has grown and I let him continue.

It's sweet, and I can't help but smile.

"Sounds good," I agree, even though I still have no idea what the fuck I'm going to do once I get to a computer.

I feel like my character Felicity in the film, "Broken Chances". She was in an accident and lost all her memories, waking up in a hospital bed 10,000 miles away from her home. She knew no one, and no one knew her. The nurse called her Felicity because that was the name of her daughter. I feel much like Felicity. A broken, lost woman in need of guidance. Silas has been my guide, but I still don't have answers. I'm scared but too afraid to show it. Please, Alexis. I hope you answer so I can go back to reality. A reality outside of this frozen, barren wasteland. My life feels fake right now. I need something to bring me back to the life I love to hate.

"Tell Anne that you're with me, she'll let you use the computers without having to buy anything," he adds as I fix my hair in the toque.

"You and Anne good friends?" I ask, thinking maybe it's an old fling after his wife left.

"She's Louisa's cousin." He tilts his head. "My ex-wife." He takes in the embarrassed look on my face. I may be a good actress, but my poker face is not the greatest. "Haven't been with anyone since Louisa," he adds as if to reassure me. I don't know why I want the reassurance but I shrug slowly.

Adrien and I had sex on New Year's Eve, just moments before people arrived at our house. That's all we do really, is screw. We make love the second we wake up, we make love after a long day of work to release some stress, and we make love to put ourselves to sleep.

Yet here I am, feeling jealous that this man beside me might have had a fling with a local after his wife. I don't even know him. Am I this fucking twisted? Or maybe I'm just horny as hell from not having sex like I'm used to. Whatever it is, I have to snap out of it.

I squeeze my eyes shut, turning away from him. "Can I ask you an extremely awkward favor?" This cold weather is doing a number on my lips and I can't stop licking them before I speak. "I don't have any underwear or a bra." Just stop, Parker, you're face is burning up enough. "I can't keep going commando in these jeans."

He laughs, spinning the keys on his finger before stuffing them in his pocket. I feel like I'm thirteen again asking my mom if I can buy thongs like all the older girls at school. At least he won't force me to say three Hail Mary's for asking such a ludicrous thing.

"Yeah, I can pick some up for you at Doreen's. What's your size?" A smirk is still spread to his lips. We've only known each other for a couple of days, but he seems less closed off than he was when we met. I don't know if having someone to talk to all day has helped or not.

"I can pick them out."

He raises an eyebrow. "There isn't much to choose from."

I sputter, looking down at my hands. "Small bottoms, thirty-four double-D for top," I answer quickly.

He smiles and gets out of the truck. "Tell Anne you're with Silas Gray."

I retreat to the little café without so much as a glance at Silas over my shoulder. My therapist will have a field day with me once I get out of this.

The café is dark red with black and gold accents; the décor feels like I walked into a burlesque show. Adrien and I went to a show a couple of years ago. He wasn't much of a fan, preferring his weekly visits with the guys to any strip club that had a VIP room. It's sad how blinded I was by Adrien. I'm beginning to wonder if maybe he just stayed with me for my success and not out of love.

There isn't anyone in the café, which makes it easier for me to record a video and take off the sunglasses. I like when coffee shops are packed with people. Writers trying to make a mark with their words, students trying to cram in as much information as they can, and businessmen and women taking a moment to breathe before they attend yet another meeting that could have been a phone call. I miss the rowdiness of New York City, and I miss the warmth of California. I want out of this. I want home. Don't I?

"Afternoon, ma'am," a woman says, flashing me a smile. Her curly hair is tucked into a cap, and her big metal glasses hang largely on her face. "What can I get you?"

"Silas Gray said I could use the computers," I answer, hoping she won't go into detail about how I know him. Though by the look she gives me as I take off his toque, she can tell I'm not lying. At least I hope so.

"Sure thing." She points to the computers by the large windows. "Passcodes are 1122."

I nod and spot today's paper on one of the tables, snagging it as I make my way to the computers. Oscar Winner, Parker Bailey, Found Dead on Canyon Road. My heart skips and sinks deep into my stomach. I shouldn't read it. I know it's a bad idea, but here I go. Unfolding it and reading through the article.

On January 1, actress, Parker Bailey, wife of Adrien Bailey, was found dead off of Canyon Road. Local authorities found her naked, beaten, and face caved in...high traces of drugs and alcohol...an investigation is still underway. What kind of trickery did Bailey get herself into?

Did I get myself into? Is this reporter for real?

Bailey has been working back-to-back on the trilogy The Beckoning...source close to the widower states that Bailey craved a much-needed break...Bailey must have finally lost it turning to drugs and alcohol...did Adrien know his wife's secret life?

I stop reading. This is stupidity. The rest of the one-page article is pretty repetitive. The journalist is going on and on about my so-called drug use and how being a hot-shot has made me turn to drugs and alcohol to cope so I wouldn't end up psychotic like some celebs who have resorted to shaving their head or losing their minds. I haven't gotten to that point yet because of Adrien. He's been my rock through everything. What am I supposed to do without my rock once this shit is over with?

One thing that I can't seem to understand is that Billy's the one who is leading the investigation in Alaska. He has a pen from Bailey Industries. Silas told me not to trust him. My guess is, whoever faked my death, Billy has something to do with it.

I let out a breath and stare at the computer screen. How am I going to do this? No one's going to believe any email I send. How can they? Adrien Bailey is one of the most powerful men in the industry and I'm just his actress wife. Shit, they might not believe me even with a webcam picture. It's pretty easy to photoshop.

All my social media accounts have been deactivated. Even my banking information doesn't work. I log into my email, and to my surprise, it works. Immediately, I change my password just in case Adrien tries to log in, too. Alexis and I sometimes chat on this when I don't want Adrien snooping through my phone. He gets jealous very easily. I usually just shove my pussy in his face to stop his mind from making up false scenarios. It always works, but that doesn't stop him from reading my messages.

I wonder if I should message my agent. It hasn't crossed my mind until now, but I opt against it. At least for now. Adrien is the one who introduced us. I don't know if I can trust her at the moment. I don't know who to trust if I'm being honest.

I find Alexis' email and stare at the cursor as it blinks at me after I type nothing but Alexis, please believe me. Oh, God, I hope she doesn't take this as a fucking prank. Or show this to Adrien. She hates him, she has to be smarter than to show him, doesn't she?

I open up the webcam and take a breath, I have no idea how I'm going to phrase this. I look up at Anne who turns on some smooth jazz and begins cleaning something. Her back is to me, which makes this whole video easier. As soon as I click record, I'm nervous, and tears are welling in my eyes.

"Alexis, a few days ago, I was found half-dead in the water and brought back to life. I don't know what the fuck is going on, or who the fuck Adrien said he did CPR on. But it wasn't me. You know me better than anyone. I don't over-abuse drugs and I surely don't drink like an alcoholic. Adrien is up to something, I don't know what, but it's something and I'm terrified to find out what it is," I pause, to remove the sunglasses and wipe my eyes. I look at the camera and inhale sharply, lifting the newspaper to the screen. "We weren't supposed to come to Alaska until my birthday. I can't remember anything from New Year's Eve and all I had was five glasses of champagne."

I let out a shaky breath and sniff, furrowing my brow. "I woke up in a cabin with the guy who helped me. He's good to me, but I don't know what to do with this shit. Adrien faked my death and I don't know why—" I lift the paper, it's shaking because of my hands. "Look, look at the date on the paper. I'm not dead. I'm not, I'm fucking scared," I groan, looking down as more tears slide down my cheeks. "Please don't show this to Adrien. I beg you, Lex. Please. Don't believe the tabloids, either. They're not true. None of it is. I'm here, Lex. I'm alive. I'm right fucking here."

I let out a breath and sniff, putting the paper in my lap and ending the recording. As soon as I slide the sunglasses back on, I sob a little more, as quietly as I can.

I upload the video to the email and hesitate before I finally click send. I hope she believes me, I really do.

Opening a new email, I write nothing more than why are you doing this to me? then send it to Adrien. I want him to be scared, I want him to know he's screwed when I figure out what to do—when I have the balls to speak to the authorities. Adrien is powerful. I can only imagine who he has in his back pocket. Talking to them now without valid proof can make what the tabloids say about me losing it become reality.

I log out of my email and be sure to delete the video. I go to empty the recycling bin on the desktop but stop. The thought of the video getting out, going viral, and then bringing more chaos my way crosses my mind. This could be a good thing. It's proof that I'm alive, but the fear that doing so will alert Adrien or whoever is involved of my whereabouts is scaring the shit out of me.

I don't delete the video.

After a few deep breaths and my failed attempts at logging into any of my social media accounts—which I might add is a fucking joke on Adrien's behalf since he doesn't even have any social media. I'm the one who posts pictures of us and promotes my films or events on them. There are so many unsaved pictures I wish I had kept copies of. Although, this new and growing hatred I have toward him is certainly masking my regret and heartache toward the loss of my memories.

The door to the café opens and he's holding a pink paper bag with a piece of paper in his hand. "Hi, Silas," Anne says.

He nods at Anne and spots me nibbling my bottom lip. A small grin touches his lips before he looks back at Anne. "Two number threes," he says, then comes to me.

"Any luck?" he asks, placing the bags on the table behind me as I close the tabs on the computer.

I adjust the sunglasses higher up my nose, handing him his toque back. "I don't know. I sent Alexis a video of me with this paper in hand. So, we'll see what happens." I tap the headline. "I also read this stupid article."

He takes the paper and glances at it. "I told you not to read it."

"Curiosity killed the cat."

He smirks, tossing the paper aside. "Mary said someone called. She didn't know who it was and they didn't say who they were looking for." He hands me the piece of paper. "Number ring any bells?"

"It's my parents' home number."

"That's a good sign."

I don't believe it. They hate me. I know they do. They told me the day I left was the day I died. That's how harshly they disowned me. It's a sad thought given that if it wasn't for Adrien sweeping me off my feet and making a name for me, I'd be crawling back home in the hopes they'd accept me.

Silas takes in the way my face darkens with regret as I stare at the piece of paper with a phone number I'll never be able to forget. "Want to try and give 'em one more call?"

I nod quickly, sniffling again, "I can try."

What good will that do?

"I'll ask Anne if you can use her phone." He slides the pink paper bag to me before he retreats.

Anne smiles as she looks up at him and nods, agreeing with whatever it is he's saying. I look at the magazine stand by the front door. My face is on every single one of the magazines.

Actress Found Dead.

Parker's Last Moments Before Death.

The Baileys mourn the loss of their son's wife.

Adrien Devastated.

Parker's Secret Life.

There are so many lies spewing from the stand. This small town is like a chapter out of hell. I feel exposed. Everyone knows everything about everyone's business. I'm in the spotlight like I've always been. I do love it. With a face like mine, who wouldn't? But right now, I wish I wasn't in the spotlight. I'm scared and I don't know who to trust. I'm in danger, but for all I know, whoever I ask can be in on it. The local sheriff is probably in on it for Chrissake!

Why the fuck did Adrien bring me here? Can't I just be in peace somewhere for once without my face and issues out in the open?

Silas returns with a cordless phone and hands it to me, a gentle grin touching his lips. I take the phone and look at it, wondering what the use is. My parents won't want anything to do with me. And even if they did, how in the hell can I convince them of the truth? They'll tell me it's the devil paying a visit for all the sins I committed in life. God striking me down.

Silas heads back to the counter and pays Anne for our lunch as I'm dialing the house number again, hoping for someone to answer, but also for it to go straight to voicemail.

After one ring, a voice I haven't heard in ten years strikes my ear.

"Hello?" Jack answers. He sounds so different. Deep voice, scratchy. My baby brother is not a baby anymore.

I never once stalked him on social media over the years. I could have. I searched his name on Instagram ninety-six times. Yes, I counted. But all I did was stare at his name and tiny profile picture that gave me nothing. Adrien encouraged me to reach out. But I couldn't. The thought of my brother hating me, makes me hate myself. So I avoided the topic. Shit, in my time of need I'm still trying to avoid it.

"Hey," I say, my breathing growing shaky.

Jack gasps. "Parker?"

"Please don't hang up."

"What the fuck's going on? Where—you don't talk to us for ten fucking years and we see on the news you're fucking dead? If this is some bullshit tabloid prank you're trying to pull, I don't want any part of it. So help me God, Mom and Dad will not be part of it, either," he bellows.

A sob chokes my air. "It's not."

His voice softens because of my cries. "What's going on?"

"I don't know. My husband and I were throwing a New Year's Eve party. The news says Adrien found me and tried to resuscitate me from drowning in the river, but that's not true! I don't know who they found and are claiming as my body. But it's not me," I weep. "I'm scared, Jacks. I'm scared and I don't know what to do." There's a silence on the other end of the line and it makes me let out a cry louder than I should've. Jack hung up on me. Of course, he did. "H-hello?"

"I'm still here, Parks," Jack says. "I don't know what to say."

"Say you believe me," I whisper.

"I do," he replies quickly. "Where are you?"

"Um." I take the paper beside me, reading out the city.

"Who're you staying with?"

"His name is Silas Gray. He saved me from the river where Adrien left me to die."

Jack sighs, groaning softly. "I don't know how I'm supposed to help. Or how I'm supposed to get to you—"

"I sent you money, I always send you money. Accept all the checks and use them, please," I beg, remembering I never wrote a date on any of the checks.

"Okay, okay. I'll...I'll figure something out. Is there a number I can reach you?"

"No, Silas doesn't have a phone...keep this number, and my email, do you remember it? You can always email me." I sniff. "I'm calling from a café. It's where the computers are."

Jack takes a breath. "Mom and Dad are worried."

I'm not sure if he's lying or telling me the truth. They hate me, don't they?

"Do they really?"

"Yes, Parks," he replies with a frustrated tone.

I sniff, knowing they deserve an apology. "I should, um, I should apologize for leaving without a note or contacting you when I got to California...I'm just...I don't know what to say."

An apology better than that.

"It's okay." He lets out a breath. "I think they forgave you long ago, just didn't know how to get in contact with you."

I let out a chuckled sigh. "Why didn't you ever accept the money I sent?"

"Mom called it the devil's money." He cracks the bones in his neck, probably wiping the back of his neck like he used to do when he was anxious. "Look, you remember Brody? Sheriff Tom's boy?"

Of course, I remember him. All he used to do was hit on me. "Why?"

"He might be able to help. He's the sheriff now, believe it or not. Is there anything you can send me as proof?" Jack asks, clicking his tongue.

I log back into my email. I open the webcam again and take a photo of myself with the phone on my shoulder and newspaper in hand, being sure to take off my sunglasses. "I just sent you a photo."

Silence blooms on the other end and I notice Silas making his way over, his eyes are so much brighter in the sunlight. It's astounding how attractive he is, but there's still that sadness looming over him like that lone rain cloud on a sunny day. He's helped me so much the last few days, I wish there's a way I can repay him.

"You look skinny," Jack says, breaking the silence.

"I have an image I have to uphold, y'know," I defend, shaking my head. "Just, please, help me if you can. I'm lost and I really don't know what to do." I take my eyes off Silas and stare at the screen. "Please, Jacks."

"I'll talk to Brody, okay?" He takes a breath. "I don't wanna hang up, but I have to. Mom's...she needs her meds."

I frown, leaning forward. "What? What do you mean?" Silas sits at the table and frowns, studying me as I try to keep it together.

"We'll talk again soon—"

I put my hand up, waving it as if he were right in front of me. "Jacks?"

He lets out a soft breath. "MS. It took hold of her and she hasn't been the same. It's not good, Parker."

Tears fall from my eyes. "Why didn't you take the money and use it to get her the help she needs?"

"She didn't want it—" he stops as a bell chimes in the distance. "I have to go. I'll email you when I can, okay? I promise I'm going to help you."

"Okay," I say softly. "I'm sorry." But he hangs up before I can finish my apology.

I let out a breath and put the sunglasses back on, desperately needing to hide my face.

"Everything all right?" Silas asks, looking at the computer, then back at me.

"Mhm." I nod. "Let's eat?"

The worry doesn't leave his face. "Get ahold of someone?"

I nod, wiping my cheeks. "Yeah, my brother."

Silas nods, sliding one of the paper bags to me, and opens our sodas. It's like he can see it on my face, I don't want to talk about it right now. "Hope you like turkey melts."

I sniff. "Yeah, they're fine."

He places a hand on mine, bringing my racing heart up to my throat. "It'll be okay, Parker."

I retract my hand and pick up open my soda that's shaking in my hand. "I hope so."

We eat the rest of our meal in silence. Not because there isn't anything to say, but because I'm on the verge of tears again. I can't fathom what Jack told me about our mother. I wasn't her biggest fan, but she's still my mom. I can't do anything to help because I'm stuck here and I haven't tried to reach out in years. I feel like if I tried, maybe she'd be okay.

Anne glances at us quite often. It's like she's not used to Silas having lunch dates with people—or Silas being with anyone at all. Or maybe she recognizes me. This could be a good thing. Or it can't be. It puts me at risk of being found by the people that tried to kill me.

I look over my shoulder and Anne looks away quickly. I don't mind it. I'm so used to people constantly staring at me, that I don't even notice Anne staring until Silas let out an annoyed sigh.

"What's wrong?" I ask, following his gaze.

"I don't like people staring."

I raise my eyebrows. "Well, do you bring people here often?"

"I never brought anyone here. I don't go on dates anymore." He smirks and lets out a chuckle. "I'm kidding."

I shake my head and bite my lip to hide my smile. "I know."

He picks up our trash. "You ready?" I nod, adjusting the sunglasses on my face. Ready as I'll ever be leaving my help in the hands of my brother I haven't spoken to in ten years.

Silas picks up our things and lets me lead us out of the café, waving at Anne before we depart.

I'm not entirely sure how I'm feeling. Perplexed, sad, hopeful? I don't even know. I spoke to my brother for the first time in ten years. He was eleven years old when I left. I was his hero, so to speak. He looked up to me in so many ways I always had this aching feeling that I let him down. I should've reached out sooner, to him at least. He must hate me as much as I hate myself for leaving him. I didn't even say goodbye.

A matte black car with flashy rims drives past. It slows for a moment, then speeds off. Odd seeing a flashy car in this town. My heart skips. Adrien. Everything's about to erupt inside of me. Screams. Cries. Bile. I won't let it out. I won't give Adrien the satisfaction of seeing me weak.

If it's even Adrien. Anyone in this town can have a flashy car like that. Silas' car is a bright red with chrome rims. A weight pushes down on my chest. Paralyzed.

I.

Can't.

Fucking.

Breathe.

My knees feel like jelly, about to give out at any second. I grip the door handle of Silas' truck to steady myself. I watch the car until I can't anymore. If it was Adrien, he would have gotten out of the car. I know he would have. He would have made a scene. It's just another tourist. Yep, that's what it is.

But the nausea hasn't subsided.

When I get in the truck, the tears start to fall. I can't control them, nor do I want to. I let my sobs out and when Silas gets into the truck and sees me crying, he sighs. I'm not sure why he does, but he puts his hand on my shoulder and leaves it there until I stop. I'm a rack of nerves and I can't help my hands from shaking. There's this lump in my throat that's growing as each day passes. All I want to do is burst it. It hurts me so much, but I don't know what else to do but wait until an answer is brought to me. What the fuck do I do?

"I'm sorry," I say through sniffs, looking over at him. Do I tell him about the car? No, it was nothing. It's nothing.

"Nothing to be sorry about."

He removes the glasses from my face and studies me for a moment, wiping a tear with his thumb. I suck in a rush of air, not expecting him to do that. His lips quirk up and he starts the truck, easing out of the spot and bringing us home.

I don't know why, but I want to talk. Maybe just to hear my voice or let the thoughts in my head out. So I do. I talk and he listens. I love the way he listens like he's in tune with everything I say. Adrien is good at that, too. At least when I spoke about something he liked. Other times, he'd just nod and agree, even though it was obvious he wasn't listening. I'd still go on as if he was. I hate silence. Maybe it's because of my upbringing. It was always quiet at home. I'd only be allowed to listen to gospel music or read books that my mother approved of. I'd steal books from the local library after school so I'd be able to read the scary and adult stuff. No one ever suspected me; being a preacher's daughter allowed me to get away with loads. I'd fill the silence with the words on the page rather than the ache to escape.

"...I never really noticed the signs until Jacks said her MS took a turn for the worst," I say, wetting my lips and staring out the window. "She used to complain about her fingers always being numb, blaming us for being brats and causing it. She'd forget things quite often, but what tired mother of two doesn't? If I didn't run away, maybe I could've helped. Or maybe if I just tried to contact them earlier in the last ten years, I could've gotten her the help she needed. I don't know. There're a lot of what-ifs running through my mind right now and I feel so fucking helpless."

I sigh softly, leaning my head back and wiping my eyes. I can't believe the woman I wished would open her fucking eyes and see a life outside of church, is now sick. This is what I get, isn't it? This is my karma for running away and forgetting about the people that raised me.

Silas adjusts his fingers on the steering wheel. "There's no reason to feel helpless. With an illness like that, there isn't much you can do aside from delay the effects."

"Guess you're right." I sniffle. "Sorry for just vomiting all this shit on you."

He gives me a quick grin. "It's no bother."

I don't think I've ever trusted someone so quickly. Maybe Adrien. The moment we met, I wanted to know everything about him. He's beautiful and I hate how beautiful he is because all I want to do now is smash his face in for hurting me.

When I first laid eyes on Silas, I thought he was beautiful, too, in this rugged, manly way. Fear and anxiety about my situation aside, he fascinates me. I have a knack for fascinating people.

This urge to put my hand on his leg as a friendly gesture swims through me. "I don't know how to thank you for every-thing." I don't put my hand on his leg.

"You don't have to thank me. It's the least I can do." He grips the steering wheel as he pulls onto his driveway, then turns to me. "I have a way you can let out some of your frustrations."

My cheeks burn up and I cover my mouth, letting out a short laugh. As attractive as he is, and as much as I would enjoy a release. I'm still married. "Silas. We barely know each other." Although the thought of him taking me roughly from behind has crossed my mind a time or two. My therapist is right and I hate that she's right.

He laughs, appreciating the humor I bring to every situation. "Not like that." His cheeks redden, too, and we stare at each other for a beat before he looks down at his rough, calloused hands. "You're married, Parker."

I don't look away from him as if the thought has crossed his mind, too. "I know."

His eyes meet mine again and smiles. I do like it when he smiles. His face brightens up and the lines around his eyes make him that much more attractive. I should be freaking the fuck out about my situation, but hearing Jack's voice made me relax. I'm getting help from someone I can trust. My baby brother. I can't believe it took this bullshit for me to grow a pair to see him again.

Silas glances at my lips, then looks out the window beside me. "Do you see that tree right there?" He points at a tree that's half out of the ground and appears as if it's about to fall over but is held up by its fellow neighboring tree branches.

"The broken one?"

He nods, wetting his lips. "It's dead, but we can use the wood for the fire. Best way to let out a little aggression is attacking something. What better way to attack something than hacking a tree to pieces?" Now I understand how he's been celibate for six years. He attacks things for a release.

I giggle. "Oh, God. You think I'm ready for a task like that?"

"Long as you don't care about breaking one of your nails," he teases.

I do, but he doesn't need to know that. So I roll my eyes instead.

Boy, is he right! We chop down the broken tree and whack at it for hours until it is in the right size pieces for the fireplace. It certainly helps me a lot. He keeps me distracted and I commend him for it.

Silas is changing me slowly but surely. He's making me realize that life doesn't revolve around a screen. I should appreciate the little things right in front of me. It's not about the designer dress or my name in the lights. It's about the here and now. The smiles and the laughs.

We sure did share a lot of laughs today. He's different, and I like different. I don't care if I'm still married. Adrien is dead to me. Our relationship died a month or so before I did. It feels nice to smile after everything that's happened. A smile I can say is one hundred percent genuine.

CHAPTE10

J olting into wakefulness as a cold hand slides to my mouth, my sleeping haze adjusts to Silas putting a finger on his lips. Marlow is barking violently downstairs, I've never heard her like this. Her savage snarls echo the home and thrills a pang of fright up my spine. Silas takes my hand and that's when I see a gun tucked into his pajama pants. He said there weren't any other guns in this house. He lied to me.

He leads us to the room that separates mine from the master bedroom. My heart aches as we step into the powder blue room with a twin bed and boxes piled in the corner. This was his son's room. Jesus, the sadness that slaps me as we move through it is painful. How can he keep all of this? The reminder alone must be heartbreaking, but physical reminders must be even deadlier.

Silas pulls me to the closet and pushes clothes out of the way, revealing a little opening he forces me into. It's dark, much too dark to even know what I'm touching or sitting on. Wearing underwear and pants right now would've been a good idea.

He gets in with me and moves some of the clothes back in place, closing us into this space. My hand touches something furry, and even though I assume it's a stuffed animal, my mind rushes to a spider's nest with dozens of spiders lingering and I just disturbed them. I imagine their little legs crawling all over me and nibbling at my skin. I grip Silas' forearm and I feel his tense body relax somewhat, knowing, I guess, he isn't here alone.

There are no spiders on me, but the creepy-crawly feeling doesn't leave. I scratch at my exposed skin a few times before he lets out a breath, causing me to stop.

Marlow's growls stop suddenly and are replaced by whimpers and yelps, making me grip Silas harder. Tears well in my eyes and slide down my nose, falling onto his shoulder. Why are they hurting her? She's doing nothing but barking. As Silas said, she's all bark and no bite.

Footfalls come to the stairs, creaking ever so lightly as they make their way to the second floor. Oh, God, they're here for me, aren't they? They want to kill me and might hurt Silas in the process. It isn't until I squeeze his arm tighter I realize that my being here might hurt him.

My heart is caught in my throat, making me whimper quietly. Silas takes a breath, touching my hand as we listen to the footfalls creeping their way into Jack's room. Boxes are shoved aside, clothes are scattered and things are knocked over.

The bed is moved, and more things are knocked over. But no one checks the closet thoroughly, only clothes are pushed aside. We're right here and they can't find us. That dark suffocating wave falls over me, causing my nails to dig into Silas' arm.

But as the footsteps retreat, my wild beating heart slowly slightly, listening in as another set of footfalls roams the rest of the house. It feels like hours that Silas and I are hiding in the little crawl space, but a mere ten minutes has passed, I'm sure of it. Ten minutes where my paper-thin nerves are at their peak.

"She's not here," a voice says as another grunts in response. Who are these people? Why are they looking for me? God-damn it, Adrien. What have you gotten us into?

A deep guttural grunt followed by a yell startles me. Silas quietly and soothingly shushes me, putting his hand on mine again. I lean my head on his shoulder, taking a few deep breaths as his thumb brushes my knuckles. The fatherly in-stinct of his shining through.

"You said this is where he lives!" A voice I know all too well rings out. Fuck you, Adrien.

"Not my fault he ain't home," another voice sounds. This one is soft and shrill.

"Parker is dead, the fuck are we still doing looking for her anyway?" a third voice says.

Adrien shrieks, over Marlow's soft whimpers. "I don't think she's fucking dead."

"And how do you know this?" the second asks.

"Funny fucking feeling," Adrien says. I don't have to see his face to know his expression. Sour like he sucked on a lemon.

"There no way in hell she could've survived the cold all naked and drugged up," the second voice continues.

The third voice grunts again. "She drowned."

"I need to see her body. I have to be sure," Adrien mentions, his voice lowers and I can barely make out the rest. "I didn't kill anyone...Parks is my wife...money talks...I still love her...hurt her." Adrien sniffs. "This wasn't my idea."

The third laughs. "The plan was enough to change the way you think, wasn't it?"

"You're the one who left my naked wife in the river," Adrien shouts. "I want—no, I need you to check every house on this side of the river. See what they're hiding, if they're hiding anyone. And I want to talk to everyone myself, so find me this Silas guy. Understood?"

"Yes, sir," the second one agrees.

"Whatever you want," the third says.

"All right," Adrien says. "Now, make this look like an accident." Their footsteps retreat.

The third laughs. "Dumbass forgot to board up the front windows."

A shuddered breath leaves me as we listen intently to what's happening. Glass shatters as if something is thrown through one of the large windows and whimpers escape Marlow once again. I keep a hand on my mouth to disguise my cries. I'm speechless. How on earth am I supposed to get away from this one? I don't understand Adrien's motive. If this wasn't his idea, then why in the hell am I supposedly dead to the world? What the fuck is going on? Why didn't he just kill me? Why leave me for dead with the chance I'd survive?

My whole body is shaking, and I can't control it. It's the fear clawing its way into my bloodstream and having a field day with my insides.

Silas reaches behind me as the house silences, his hand grazing my bottom. He ignites a small dinosaur flashlight. I'm sure my cheeks are stained with the mascara I forgot to remove last night, my teeth are chattering, and I'm shaking. Fuck, I can't stop shaking. The pit of my stomach is in knots and I'm going to be sick.

It's okay, he mouths. But that just eats away at my nerves even more because he's so fucking calm. Why is he so calm?

A storm brews deep within me and I know I'm going to hit my boiling point soon. I don't know how much longer I can take the constant fear that someone is going to find me and going to kill me right this time. It's been two days since we last went into town and I spoke to my brother. Going back isn't a good idea at this point, but if he can help me get out of this hell I'm living in, then I'll have to chance it. Adrien, what are you doing?

Thundering footfalls leave the house and an engine turns over, its vibrating rumble disappears from the grounds. Silas keeps the flashlight on us, waiting patiently as his other hand grips the gun. I don't notice until he moves to fix the gun in his pants that half-moon ridges from my manicured nails are dug into his skin. One of them is bleeding, too.

The greenish light shuts off and my heart hammers violently. I hate the dark. I always have. I'm almost twenty-seven years old and the dark is something I fear the most in this world.

"What're you doing?" I whisper, gripping his shirt as he takes off the opening of the crawl space.

"I'm going to scope the house," he whispers back.

"Don't leave me in here."

I can see the contemplation in his gaze. I can't tell if he heard more of what they said than I did. But Adrien was here for me. How in the hell does he know who Silas is, is another question all on its own. Sheriff Billy must've said something and clicked his Bailey's Industries pen while doing it.

I don't want Silas hurt in the end. He saved me when he didn't have to and is still taking care of me when he doesn't need to. I fear something might happen and there doesn't seem like there's anything I can do but leave and try to find a safe haven when I can.

"Then stay close," Silas states, standing upright in the closet.

The bedroom has been ransacked. Boxes are knocked over, the twin bed is moved, and toys and clothes scatter the floor. One box that was knocked over, is open to photos of smiling faces. It pains me to see the beautiful boy he lost to stupidity. If only Silas knew the hunting laws around here, that poor boy would never be in the line of fire.

Silas raises the gun as we move through the upper floor. The bedroom I'm staying in is in shambles, clothes, blankets, and pillows are thrown around the room. Nothing too hectic compared to little Jack's room.

I'm still holding onto Silas' shirt and he reaches back to take my hand, interlocking our fingers. I've gotten to know him, not well enough to hold his hand, but I am and there isn't an ounce of discomfort. I've filmed many scenes where I'd have to hold onto someone, kiss someone, or make fake love to someone, and nothing was ever this comforting.

The floorboards creak under our feet thrumming panic through me, but there's no one in the house anymore that can hear it. At least I hope there isn't. I've filmed enough scary movies to know that the killer is always lurking in the shadows.

My grip on his hand tightens when I look behind me at the open door of his room. Darkness stares back at me, it's cold and lifeless. How can he sleep in the pitch blackness? The fire was quietly crackling in my room when I fell asleep, giving off that perfect glow I needed. But his room?

I see it again. That lanky shadowy figure with one too many unnaturally angled arms—stop. It isn't real. Take a breath, Parker. Work through your fear.

Marlow whimpers when she sees Silas and he drags me to her, forcing me to my knees. The poor thing is crying. She doesn't deserve this. Silas doesn't deserve this fear. These people are after me, and yet I feel like I made Silas part of this fucked up problem.

"She's bleeding," I say quietly through a cry.

"Stay with her," he demands and continues through the house.

I pet her gently, feeling her shaky breath as she tries to move. I avoid touching her open wounds. I don't know what they did to her but I hope it isn't too bad. Silas has lost enough, he doesn't need to lose Marlow, too.

I peer outside, trying to see in the darkness, but all I see is my wild imagination conjuring up my demons. Dark shadows lurk in the distance, swaying side to side as they make their way to us. Their feet touch the snow, but no footprints to depict their whereabouts. I swear I can hear the crunch of their boots on the snow, I can see the clouds of smoke in the air, and piercing eyes sparkle in the darkness. It isn't real because nothing is there. Darkness greets me on the other side.

A scream rumbles deep within me, but it won't come out. The longer I look outside, the more realistic my demons are becoming.

Silas' hand moves to my shoulder and I jolt, looking up at him. I'm sure my eyes are puffy and red. "No one's here,' he reassures, looking down at Marlow and putting the safety on his gun. "Hey, girl. You all right?"

She lets out a sigh and blinks slowly.

"Is there an animal hospital close by?" I ask through a sniff.

"No."

My eyebrows furrow. "A vet?"

He nods, scanning her wounds. "Mm, they open at eight."

"I'm sorry." I'm not sure what else to say at this point.

He pets Marlow and inspects her wounds closely. "Not your fault."

"If I wasn't here and didn't call Adrien, he wouldn't come looking for me." I wipe my eyes. "How did he know I was here?"

"Told you Billy wasn't someone to trust," Silas says, rubbing his nose on the top of his wrist. "People keep seeing me with someone in town. I never bring anyone around, people get to talking, and I'm thinking some people might recognize you."

"H-how do you know this?"

He sighs, sitting back on his feet. "Towns folk said so when we went into town two days ago."

"Why didn't you tell me? I wouldn't have been around you or gone into town with you," I scoff, wiping my cheeks. "Is that why Anne kept looking at me?"

He doesn't look at me. "You've been in contact with your brother, we have to go into town together."

I sniff, wiping my eyes again as a shiver moves through me. It's fucking cold outside tonight. There isn't a bone in my body that isn't shaking right now. I'm scared. I'm tired. And I'm fucking freezing. I just want to go home. Even though there's no home left for me to go to.

"I can't believe Adrien came here...some birthday, huh?" I let out a soft chuckle and immediately frown. He glances up at me and catches my eye. My teeth are chattering, but I keep my mouth closed so he doesn't notice—which he does. He notices everything. "Do you think Billy told them or maybe Anne?"

"If they're asking people around town." He takes an annoyed breath as he looks at Marlow. "Then anyone could have said something."

This is probably how Adrien knows who Silas is. How he found him, too. And if he found him it's only a matter of time before Adrien and his men find me. God only knows what they'll do to me when they do.

He wets his lips, finally meeting my eyes. "How much is your life insurance?" His facial expression doesn't change from an aggravated and menacing look.

"More than what I make in a year."

"Which is?"

I shrug. "The insurance gives him everything I own. All my rights in the industry, all my royalties, all the properties...and a lump sum of roughly half a billion dollars. Why?"

Silas releases a breath, shifting his gaze to Marlow. "Motive."

Marlow wheezes and I'm beginning to think she may not make it through the rest of the night. Fuck, I feel like shit right now.

He rises again, taking the blanket from the couch and wrapping Marlow in it. She yelps, as he wraps her but it doesn't seem like she is in too much pain, just exhausted. He lifts her and brings her to the couch, petting her head softly.

The front window on the right of the door is broken, and cold air is seeping in quickly with billowing snow clouding in circles as it swarms on the wooden floors. My exposed toes are beginning to sting. I'm shaking like a glass of water during an earthquake and my chattering teeth have a mind of their own.

Silas looks up at the shattered glass. "Mm."

"Say something," I whisper.

"We should get some sleep. We gotta leave early to bring her to the vet."

I shake my head, but it makes no difference. I'm already shaking profusely because of the fear coursing through my veins. "Leave early? How can you think of sleep right now?"

"There's nothing I can do about Marlow, there's nothing I can do about the window, and there's fuck all I can do about your husband—"

"I should leave," I interrupt.

He raises his hands and drops them at his sides. "And go where?"

My shaking hand wipes my cheek. "Somewhere that doesn't put you in harm's way."

He stares at the broken glass on the floor. 'There ain't nowhere you can go."

"It's been two days since I last spoke to my brother, I can try him again, see where that gets me," I suggest, clenching my hands into fists at my sides.

He shakes his head quickly. "You don't need to leave."

"I feel like I should," I whisper. I also feel like he's keeping me here, trying to hide me from the world he deems unsafe. I know it isn't safe, but I have to venture out there to find a solution.

"She'll be fine," he says, looking down at Marlow.

Without another word, he tosses a few logs into the fire, poking them so the flames rage into action. I watch him, wondering what's going through his head. He seems distraught, but also calm. How can he be calm in a situation like this? I'm still shaking and not just because I'm freezing.

He pokes at the logs, getting lost in them like something's on his mind. Tell me for fuck's sake!

Goosebumps form on my skin from another gust of wind. Goddamn, my nipples feel like razor blades against the cotton fabric of his shirt. I don't think I've ever been this cold. "Why do you have so many guns?" I gulp. He said he owned one gun.

He pokes the fire, watching the dancing flames for a beat. "You're not the only one with skeletons in their closet."

"I don't have any skeletons."

"Your husband sure does."

I fold my arms across my chest and look out at the darkness once more. Mocking me. It's easy to lose it in a place like this. Seclusion can lead to several problems. And I can already feel myself tiptoeing close to the brink of insanity. Sadly, I can't even blame it on the seclusion or the fuckery my husband is playing on me. It's the movies I film. The characters I'm forced to become to be the amazing actress that I am. They are what's making me lose it. Everything else is just icing on the cake.

I let out a breath watching as it clouds in front of me. "What do we do?"

He doesn't even look at me. He stares at the fire as if the answer is within it. "I don't know."

"Then I should leave. I've done nothing but put you out and take your money for things I won't need once I'm out of here." My chattering teeth are making it hard to talk normally. If I wasn't such a dumbass, I would've moved from my spot. But I don't. I stand here feeling my toes and legs begin to burn from the cold.

He shoots a look at me. "It's not safe."

"It's not safe here, either," I whisper.

He wipes a hand down his face, tightening his jaw. "I can protect you."

It feels like he needs to do this somehow. As if protecting me is a way to redeem himself for not taking care of his son when he needed it most.

How can I even compare us right now? This cold is messing with my brain.

My shoulders tense and my body starts to shake. "Do taxis come to this town?"

He shoots another glare at me. "Stop."

"No, I should—I have to leave. I don't want you to get hurt. Christ, look what they did to Marlow because of me," I manage, convulsing without realizing it.

He glances at Marlow. Her deep breaths let us know she's okay. I don't know the severity of her injuries and I sure hope Adrien's men didn't hurt her that badly. "Let's...let's get some sleep and think it over in the morning."

"Sleep?" I scoff and start for the stairs, stopping halfway up and turning back to him. He's still staring at me, taking in the fact that I'm just wearing his t-shirt and nothing else. "How can you think of sleep right now?"

He takes his wool sweater and places it on top of Marlow. "I'll be down here 'til morning. No one'll come in—"

"I don't think I can sleep alone," I blurt out and push my lips together. What're you stupid? Go upstairs and sit in the damn fireplace to warm up. Barricade the door. Don't show him you're scared to sleep alone. "Sorry...never mind."

"Mm," he grunts.

I shake my head and continue up the stairs to the room I've made mine. I pick up whatever was knocked over, putting clothes, blankets, and pillows back in place. There isn't a lock on the door, but I know closing it will make me feel better. You can hear a pin drop in this house, so no one will be able to get close enough without me grabbing the knife I keep under my pillow.

I crawl under the covers, looking out the window right by the bed. Frost consumes the edges, creating a beautiful border of unique designs. Everything is dark outside. Not a single flicker of light or a glow to signify any form of life in the dense hibernating forest. We are truly secluded.

The chills don't leave me, my body is shaking and chattering under the covers. I bring my knees to my chest and curl the covers up to my nose to warm myself with my breath. Nothing is working. I can barely feel the tips of my toes anymore. The fire is dying as well. Shit, I need to feed it but I can't move. I have never been this fucking cold in all my life.

I hear Silas' footfalls making their way upstairs. He moves to his room, then toward mine, but stops and takes a couple of steps back before he continues. I can hear the contemplation in his pacing. The door to my room opens and closes. Silas sighs when I turn to him and he takes a few logs from the floor, tossing them in the fire. He pokes it until the flames roar but doesn't say anything.

I turn back to the window, knowing that this will probably be my last night here. Happy fucking birthday to me.

Silas clears his throat, but I don't turn to him. The covers are up to my nose and I'm still shaking. Quietly, he peels his shirt off, tossing it at the end of the bed, and lifts the covers behind me.

"What're you doing?" I ask, feeling his body press up against mine.

"By the time the heat makes it here, you'll freeze to death."

I don't say anything as his hand slides to my side while the other curls up onto the pillow behind me so he could rest his head. My breathing is erratic, I don't understand why he's making me so nervous. We're known each other for a few days now. The fright that surrounded him when we first met has nearly diminished and I've grown to trust him. Yet as his heavy breathing caresses my ear, my body stiffens. He's helped me in so many ways. I trust him with my life, yet being this close to me is irking the pit of my stomach.

He isn't wrong, though. His body heat is definitely helping my shivering.

"I'm sorry," I whisper, sinking into his ridged embrace.

His arm moves from my side and slithers to my stomach, resting his hand on the bed. He doesn't speak, only exhales shakily. I feel his legs curl up behind me, pressing into my backside and against my hamstrings. My shivering isn't as tense anymore. It's really helping.

I've never been this anxious or nervous around a man—well, aside from Jedediah. We attended the same Sunday school in Vermont. He was an outsider like me, wanting nothing more than to make our own choices when it came to religion rather than have it shoved down our throats.

On May 25, twelve years ago when I was only fifteen and he was seventeen, I gave him the one thing I was supposed to save for marriage in one of the confessionals. We fooled around for the better part of the year every Sunday until he graduated high school and got out of dodge. We stayed in touch from time to time and still do today. He goes by Jed now thanks to me and constantly brags to everyone that he was the first person to sleep with Parker Bailey. Jed leaked photos of the two of us when we were teenagers and it was all over the news. Every magazine, every website. Just Jed and me in our glory. I should've been mad, heck I could've sued him if I wanted. But I didn't.

Seeing those photos reminded me of simpler times, not the fifteen minutes of fame Jed got and the butt load of money from the magazines. If only I knew his number, maybe he'd help me out, too, for a price.

"Happy birthday, Parker," Silas whispers, his body growing heavy.

I still can't understand how he can sleep right now. Yet knowing he's here with me, brings me an ounce of safety in this fucked-up chapter of my life.

CHAPTER 11

I wake to the sounds of Marlow whining loudly. Silas is still holding me, it seems we didn't move at all last night. I don't mind it, either. I like the safety I feel in his robust arms and tall physique.

As soon as Marlow's cries meet his ears, he jumps out of bed and quickly leaves as if we were about to get caught. I understand. I doubt he's been this close to a woman since his wife left—what was it six years ago? Jeez, it's been like seven days and I don't know what I'd do without the touch of someone—pleasurable or not, just to have someone to talk to every day is a necessity.

Our first task of the day is getting Marlow to a vet. I hope she's okay. I'd hate myself if something were truly wrong. If only I could pay for it, I'd have her looked at by the best of the best.

"Morning," I say, folding my arms as the main floor is a helluva lot colder than the upper floor. He must've boarded the broken window quickly before coming to bed, yet it is still cold as hell.

He places his arms in the puffy vest. "Hi." He doesn't look at me. Maybe he feels the awkwardness as I do.

I step over to Marlow. "How is she this morning?"

"Think one of her ribs is broken," he replies, handing me his jacket. "I'll get her in the truck."

I follow him out of the house and hop into the truck. He's still not saying anything, and it's starting to bother me. It shouldn't, but it does. He's hot, I'll give him that, and I know I'm attractive. That's one of the reasons I wanted out of the small town I grew up in. People deserve to see this face. Maybe he wanted more last night? No, that can't be it. We just got scared, the house was cold, we were half-naked in b ed...maybe I just need a good dicking to calm my freaked-out and twisted-up mind.

*

We drive through the town, then outside, where the veterinarian lives. We pull up to the large glass-enclosed house. It's fucking gorgeous and entirely out of place from the usual cabins and homes around here.

Horses, chickens, pigs, a few sheep, and llamas roam the grounds in a wooden gated enclosure. I look back at Marlow, she's breathing softly and looking around as if trying to distract herself with whatever she can see rather than the pain she's in.

He clears his throat, looking up at me. "On the way back we'll stop at the café to use the computers."

I sniff, wiping my nose on the sleeve of the jacket. "Okay."

"You feeling all right this morning?" he asks, staring at my lips.

I shake my head, looking at my hands in my lap. "Like shit for putting you through this."

He hesitantly touches my leg, tapping twice. "I told you, it's no bother."

My eyes well with tears. "I still think I should leave."

"Where're you gonna go?" he scoffs, removing his hand.

"I don't know?" I sniffle, looking at Marlow, then meeting his jade eyes. "He tried to kill me and then broke into your house and hurt your dog. God, who knows how many other people he's done this to who live around you." I wipe roughly at my cheeks. "Or who knows, maybe he'll come back."

It takes everything in him to say this. "At least find a place to go if you wanna leave."

"It's not that I wanna leave. I just don't want you to get hurt." I shake my head. "You saved my life, the last thing I need is for you to get hurt."

He bores into my eyes. "I'll be all right, you don't have to worry about me." He's so intimidating, I wish I could swim in his thoughts just to understand him better. It's a need at this point to know everything about him. One is about the guns.

"Why do you have so many guns?"

He takes a breath and looks out the windshield. I wonder what he's thinking. The way his tongue moves along his bottom lip makes me want to shake him. He does this every time I say something he doesn't like. Maybe if he answered my damn questions, I wouldn't say things that annoy him so much.

"Well, when you're as successful as I was, there's gonna be some things you gotta do to stay on top," he answers, gripping the top of the steering wheel with one hand while the other rests on his leg. He looks like we're driving down the highway, keeping his gaze out in front of us and in that comfortable yet alert position. "I've done some bad things for some bad people. I own them guns to protect my fam—myself in case they come back." He turns to me and tries to keep his face expressionless, but it's those eyes that give him away. The menacing secrecy they hold—he's done some terrible things I can't even begin to imagine. He was a lawyer, what kind of bad things can a lawyer get into? "That's the only reason."

"Wh-who did you do bad things for?"

He groans, dropping his grip on the steering wheel. "The Belizzos."

My breath catches in my throat. Who the fuck is this guy? Is he insane? Does he have a death wish? The Belizzos are Italian mobsters who would kill their own kids to get what they want. Adrien deals with them we've gone to business dinners, eaten at their restaurant, and attended their daughter's christening.

I'm out of breath all of a sudden, gulping thickly. "What did you do?"

"Need to know basis," he says, nodding at a man who begins making his way towards us.

I grip his forearm, wincing. "I think I need to know if you want me to stay with you until—until whatever this bullshit is can be solved."

He looks at me, that tongue moving along his bottom lip, and nods. A nod I know means he'll tell me when he's ready. I'm ready and I want to know now.

"Morning, Silas," the man says, knocking on Silas' window. Silas smiles and gets out of the truck. Quickly, I slide the sunglasses on and make for the other side.

Silas gestures toward me. "Marty, this is a friend of mine from back home."

Please don't recognize me. Please don't recognize me. Please don't recognize me. Please don't—

Marty gives me a quick once-over and smiles. "Morning, little lady."

Folding my arms in this enormous jacket, I smile back. "Hi."

Marty turns his attention to Silas. "What can I help you with?"

"Marlow hurt herself last night. Let her out to do her business," Silas pauses and strains, picking up Marlow. "I think she busted a rib."

"I'll have her looked at," Marty says, scratching behind Marlow's ear. "How you doing, girl?" Marlow barks and lets out a whine.

Silas cocks his head at me to follow him as Marty leads us to the building beside the main house. It's exactly what a veterinarian's office should look like, except it's not in a city, it's in the middle of butt-fuck nowhere.

The stale blue walls are chipping near the ceiling. Different styled chairs scatter the entrance—a waiting room with no clear theme. There's a metal and wooden desk with a chair and a laptop sitting at the far end by a door that I assume leads to the exam rooms. Large and long file cabinets crowd behind the metal desk, some drawers are left open, some folders are piled on top and some sitting on the floor. It's extremely unorganized. Barkley's veterinarian's office was the complete opposite of this. It was a bright yellow office with picture frames of different animals, magazines, and books sat on side tables between the chairs with information on cats and dogs. There was a secretary who always gave me lollipops and knew all the pets by name. This place looks run-down and abandoned compared to that.

Marty taps the table and smiles at her as Silas places her on an exam table in the furthest room down the small corridor. "All right, girl, let's get you fixed up, hmm?"

She lets out whines, whimpers, and yelps. I can barely hold it together as Marty is pushing her sides and moving her joints. I step out of the room for some air in this insanely freezing ass town. It snows constantly yet people are totally fine with it. They're always so cheery and eager to say hi. Back home, everyone minds their business. In the industry I work in, people fake their smiles and hellos to be on your good side. But here, they actually want to say hi to you. I hate the nosiness here. And all this friggen snow.

I'm pacing the front yard, adjusting the sunglasses Silas loaned me, and trying to figure out a plan.

Go home and show my face to the world, which would put Adrien in jail and give me all the money he has. But the downfall is I could literally be killed for real this time. Hope my brother, Jack, figures out what to do and doesn't take this as a way to screw me over for leaving ten years ago. Grow a pair and call my agent—who is tied to Adrien—and see if she'll help me out. Everything backfires and I'm stuck here forever.

That's all I can come up with. I try to find different solutions, but what the fuck else am I supposed to come up with? They broke into Silas' house last night and hurt Marlow. That could have been him. Shit, that could have been me.

Then again, staying here with Silas might not be that bad. He's hot as fuck in that dark, lumberjack "I have a secret" kind of way. I feel like I can fix him. More importantly, he's extremely kind and so generous. I wouldn't know how to say bye without feeling like an asshole for everything he's done for me. And who are we kidding, I can use a friggen break.

Being famous isn't as awesome as people think it is. It's straining, stressful, and aggravating. I can't go anywhere without trying to hide from the paparazzi or fans. I can't remember the last time Adrien and I had a moment of peace. I hate to admit it, but I'm kind of enjoying this break from reality. For eight years, my face has been posted all over the world. My films have been seen by millions of people. I can't remember a day that hasn't gone by where my life isn't made up by those celebrity magazines. A break. I can really use this break.

Some fucking twenty-seventh birthday this is, huh?

"Hey," Silas calls and makes his way to me with a bill in hand.

I adjust the sunglasses again, sniffling. "Is she okay? What's going on?"

He folds the bill and places it in his back pocket. "Marty's keeping her for a couple days. Needs X-rays, a cast, and other things. She'll pull through in the end."

There's no way he's paying for this when I caused it. "Whatever the bill is. I'll pay for it when I get access to my money again."

"Marty owes me a favor, just had to pay for the consult, everything else is fine." Silas waves his hand in the air. "Don't worry about it."

"You say that a lot."

He places his hand on my back. "C'mon, I gotta pick up some things at the market and you gotta check out the café."

"Are we going to finish the conversation we started?"

He drags in an annoyed breath. "Soon."

He gets into the truck and turns the engine over, not even giving me the chance to buckle my belt before he's already backing up and turning onto the main road. The drive is quick and quiet. It's always quiet with him.

He parks in front of the café and hands me a five-dollar bill for some coffee for us before he jogs over to the market. The one owned by Mary.

My mind is running a mile a minute as I approach the café. I wonder what I'll see, what I'll open. Fuck, please be something good. I need out of this town. I miss home. I miss my bed. I miss my phone. As much as I like being away from my chaotic life, I miss my rituals. Waking up and putting my face on with creams that have no business being that expensive. Reading my scripts. Watching Netflix. Wiggling my toes in the sand. I don't miss the paparazzi, the screaming fans, or the hectic hours I have to spend filming. God, I will not miss any of that. But the smell of salt in the air. The feeling of the sun on my face. I'll never get tired of that.

Anne is reading a romance novel at the counter. Her thick eyebrows are furrowed and she looks like she's about to cry. I can't remember a time a book did that to me. Damn, I don't think a book ever did that to me. Come to think of it, I don't even think I've read a book to completion in the last five years. I read a page or two here and there. If I get bored, I start a new one. But with the scripts I'm given and the hours I have to spend reading and rereading them...life gets in the way.

I don't even think my attention span can focus for more than thirty seconds because of my love for my cell phone. Shit, I miss scrolling endlessly through my social media. Checking those box office numbers. And making TikTok's. It's a wonder how I've lasted a week without it.

Anne sniffs and puts her book face down. 'Computers again?" she asks as I approach the counter.

"Two coffees, too."

"For you and Silas?" she pries.

"Yep."

A smirk touches her lips. "You and Silas been together long?" She takes to-go cups for us.

"Uh—"

She giggles. "He hasn't brought anyone around since Louisa."

"Oh"

"Don't hurt him, okay?"

I turn my attention away from her as a few locals walk by. "Wasn't planning on it."

"How do you like your coffee?" she asks, changing topics rather quickly.

"Black, one sugar," I answer, looking at the computers now. "Mind if you bring them to me?"

"Of course. Would you like some muffins, too? Just made them."

I place the five-dollar bill on the counter. "I only have five dollars on me."

"Any friend of Silas is a friend of mine." She takes the five-dollar bill and bags two muffins for us. Well, maybe I'm overreacting because I hate winter. Aside from the nosiness, maybe this town isn't half bad. It's my breather from life.

"Thanks."

Quickly, I sit at the same computer and enter my email information. Patiently waiting for the web browser to load. The internet is almost as shitty as dial-up.

Thirty new emails. Fuck yeah!

Most of them, from what I see, are from producers, celebrity friends, and a couple of directors. They're wishing me happy birthday and giving their sob story about how much they hate themselves for taking life for granted and not appreciating the time we shared—these are the modern-day letters they think I'll never be able to read. Half of these dumb wits actually believe I'm dead.

Then there are the few that don't trust Adrien, saying he's covering something up. I wonder if I should write those back, the ones who don't think I'm gone. It's a long shot, but it could work, couldn't it?

Six coworkers. That's how many emails I hit the reply button on. I share a photo of me holding a copy of the local paper. Do whatever you can. I am not dead. Adrien set me up. Please, help me. I hit send on each of them with that exact statement. I feel like I'm holding my breath, hoping for the best.

I stop on an email from Jed, and a smile touches my lips. You were my one and I let you go. Now there will never be the opportunity to tell you this. Happy birthday, Parks. I love you and I wish we could start over back when we were kids in those confessionals. It's sweet and to the point. I don't think I felt that love for Jed as I thought I did. It was just puppy love and the moment another dick was inside me, I forgot all about him. He'll always be my friend, but nothing more than that. I star the email, saving it for later.

I search for Alexis or Jack's email. Alexis wrote back with nothing more than Are you for real? I don't know what to make of it, so I reply with the same picture I sent out to the six people. I'm for real, Lex. This shit is fucked-up, but please help me.

I want Jack to write me back. He'll help, I know he will. But there isn't an email from Jack. Just my luck, isn't it?

I log out again, knowing it's no use right now. It's been a couple of days since we last spoke, you figure Jack would've at least given me an update on today of all days. What? Still mad at me that you can't give your big sister a happy birthday message? Gah, I'm being petty but I'm going stir-crazy in this town.

I don't notice it, but as I'm pinching the bridge of my nose, the glasses lift, making Anne see more of my face than she needs to see.

"Hey...you look just like—" Anne stops as the bell at the door chimes and Silas walks in with a brown paper bag in his arms.

"Morning, Anne," he says, looking at me as I rise and take the coffees and muffins from her.

I put my head down, walking out of the café. "Thanks for the muffins."

"Hi, Silas." She looks at me, then back at him. "Where did you meet your friend?"

"Long story." He chuckles. "See you later."

"Wait, Silas. Is she—"

"We're late, Anne. Had to take Marlow to the vet," Silas interrupts. There we go. Another person recognized me. Shit, I have to get out of town fast before word spreads. I don't want Adrien to find me.

"Have a good day now," she calls out to us and watches from the windows.

I don't say anything until I'm in the truck and sinking into the seat. Even then, what comes out makes no sense it's all. Stutters and stammers instead of words. Silas looks at me with raised eyebrows as I try to speak. Yep, I sound like I'm speaking another language, don't I?

"Wanna try that again?" he asks with a short laugh.

"I think she recognized me."

He shakes his head. "Anne can't tell the difference between a red light and a green light. She's one helluva coffee maker, though, but she's as dumb as a doorknob. You'll be fine."

"How can you be so sure?"

He cocks his head at the bag on my lap. "Look how she spells carrot muffins."

I can't help but laugh. Karat Muffins is written in black marker. He wasn't wrong. If this is how she spells something as simple as carrot muffins, then there's no way she recognized me. Right?

Fuck! I can't stop thinking that maybe Adrien is still here. Waiting for me to show up somewhere and kill me when no one's watching. I've never been this paranoid in all my life and I smoked pot for the better part of my early twenties.

We pull up to Silas' house and I feel like crap again when I see the broken window. He quickly boarded it up last night with plywood he had around the yard, being sure to secure it with nails poking out because of the bears and wolves around here.

"I'm going to take a shower if that's okay?"

"I'm gonna be fixing the window a little better anyway." The second our eyes meet, he smiles largely and looks down at his hands before back up at me. Ouff, he's cute right now. How can someone so cute have lived such a tragic life and have so many secrets?

I can't help but smile back. "What?"

"Happy birthday," he says and hops out of the truck.

This year is so different than any other year. There's no extravagant party. No booze. No drugs. No expensive dress that barely covers my body. No party guests who don't give a shit about me but want to be part of the celebration. There's just me and Silas, a man I've gotten to know a little but want to know so much about. It's different this year, and I think I'm going to like it.

Happy birthday to me.

CHAPTER 12

We mind our business most of the day. He's fixing the broken window and I'm roaming the upper floor in his oversized t-shirt after my shower, cleaning up the mess Adrien's goons made. When I come across his son Jack's room, I feel unwelcomed in it but clean it up anyway. Silas doesn't need to do this himself, he doesn't need the reminder of the most important thing in his world snatched away from him.

I pick up box after box and suddenly feel a hand on my shoulder. I jump and nearly fall into the box of Legos. Silas grabs my arms and helps me stand. "You, just—you don't have to clean this room. Anything but this room."

"S-sorry, I thought it would be better if I did this so you wouldn't have to see or touch his things."

Silas is still holding onto my arms. "I appreciate it. But, uh, come downstairs. Dinner's ready." He gives the room a quick scan before meeting my eyes again.

I nod quickly, and that's when he releases me.

I'm stunned when I come downstairs. He made me a candlelight dinner with a glass of red wine, spaghetti and meatballs, and a small cake with unlit candles on the table for dessert. There's a bottle of rum on the coffee table I assume is for later. This is the most romantic gesture anyone has ever done for me. I literally have no words.

I place a hand on my chest in total and utter shock. "Silas, what's all this?"

"As shitty as your situation is, it's still your birthday, Parker," he says, helping me to my seat beside him.

I sit down and am unable to hide my smile. "You didn't have to do this."

"Just like you didn't have to clean my son's room," he adds and sits down. "Again, as shitty as this situation is, you still deserve a birthday."

I can't stop smiling. "Well, thank you."

"Mm, any time," he says, scooping pasta into my plate, then his.

"Something From Nothing" playing in the background, which helps fill the silence. I forgot how cute this song is. The first time I heard it, Adrien and I were sitting in the sand having a drink. It came onto his shuffle and he instantly jumped to his feet, pulling me up to dance with him. I have the sudden urge to do the same thing with Silas right now. But I won't, not yet.

The spaghetti sauce is sweet, so much better than any five-star or Michelin-star restaurant I've ever been to. It reminds me of my mother's cooking. She loved making stuffed pasta shells for the church lunch every Sunday. She'd spend hours preparing the sauce, stuffing the shells. and slowly cooking everything before church Sunday mornings. I'd have so many of those shells she nearly slapped me upside the head for taking more than I should and not allowing others to have any. I don't think Silas would mind if I went for seconds.

"So," I say, wiping my mouth.

He grunts, reaching over for the bottle of red and filling my glass again before his. "Mm?"

"Can you tell me what you meant before?" I spin pasta onto my fork. "What did you do for the Belizzos?"

He lets out a soft chuckle, taking a sip of his wine as he watches me eat. I hate when people watch me eat. I already have the world watching me, I don't need them to do it when I'm doing something intimate like eating.

"Do you know who they are?"

"I do."

He licks some sauce from the corner of his mouth. "Well...I was their lawyer."

"That's it?"

He chuckles softly. "No."

I gulp some wine. "Then spill."

He spins the wine in his glass and contemplates what to say for a moment. I can see it in his eyes he's thinking of the right thing to say, and of course, that tongue slides along his bottom lip.

The corner of his lips curls up slightly. "Well, they funneled money through my bank account so it would come out clean when I transferred it back. We made it look like we were doing business together with simple things like a new metal fence around my house, a new paving stone driveway, and granite counters in my kitchen. They'd do all this work and I'd transfer them the money they funneled to me."

"Didn't it look fishy seeing hefty chunks of change go into your bank account?"

"I'd pretend to represent them as clients. They'd give me cash and I'd write out a phony bill with whatever amount on it...it was easy money until people started to notice. My ex-wife being one of them. She threatened to turn me in and take Jack away. So, I stopped. Stopped accepting their calls, turned them away at the office with security, and eventually, packed up all my things when they started making house calls. We moved out here to get away from that bullshit, well, planned to before Jackie died. Antonio Belizzo wasn't too pleased when I up and left. That's why I keep guns around the house," he confessed, gulping his wine. "There's one taped behind your headboard."

The Belizzos are almost as bad as the Baileys, except the Baileys are very secretive about what they do to stay on top. There are no blood trails, no witnesses. One of the reasons I don't know anything about anything.

"Told you we all have skeletons in our closet," Silas adds, taking a lavish bite of his meatball.

"You think your wife would ever give you up?"

"My ex-wife," he corrects as if hearing it from me bothers him. "No, I don't think so. It's been six years since I last saw her. I can assume she's cleaned me from her life for good."

I chuckle, taking the glass of wine and lifting it to him. "To shitty exes."

"Don't think your husband is your ex yet," he says, clinking my glass regardless.

I gulp the rest of the wine in the glass. "He tried to have me killed, I think that merits the ex title." He doesn't know it, but I'm a lightweight and I'm already starting to feel that weightless tingling feeling I get when I drink.

He drains his glass and sets it down, licking the remnants from his lips. "I don't understand why he didn't cut you in on the deal. Half a billion dollars is a lot of money. If he still loves you, then why not cut you in on it?"

"I wonder the same thing," I say quietly. "Probably doesn't love me as much as he says he does."

Silas doesn't say anything and finishes off the bottle of wine, opening the next one to fill our glasses again. I feel my cheeks start burning, I'm definitely feeling it, but I need this. Everything going on has given me so much more anxiety and paranoia. If it wasn't for Silas, I don't know what I'd do.

I never realized how much we have in common. Our likes and dislikes are almost the same. We both like dogs over cats. Thrillers and horror movies over sappy rom-coms and dramas. We're night owls, cursing those who wake up at the crack of dawn. And Halloween is our favorite holiday, to name a few. His music taste is questionable but to each their own.

He didn't always want to be a lawyer. Growing up, he wanted to be a cop like his father was. Something changed he says, and when he applied to Harvard Law School, he got in without question and chose to represent those who needed help. Somewhere along the way, his decision-making changed and that was around the time he started representing the Belizzos.

We polish off two bottles of wine and clear the table before moving to the couch to have some cake. I take two glasses from the shelf and open the rum, I'm getting hammered tonight and no one's going to stop me. It's my friggen birthday and my life is complete shit. I need this more than anything.

He chuckles, bringing the small chocolate cake with vanilla frosting and colorful sprinkles to me. A single candle in the middle of the cake is lit behind his hand. "Well, I ain't gonna sing happy birthday because I don't have the best singing voice."

I'm smiling so big my cheeks hurt. "You didn't have to do this."

I have no words. I'm so touched and thankful. I might actually cry right now.

He sits beside me and holds the cake closer. "Least I could do." I see two forks in the palm of his hand and giggle softly. His eyes are so beautiful by the light of the fire I can't help but gaze into them as I think of a wish. My only wish is to find that happiness I thought I had. Not to go home, just to find that glee again. I blow out the candle and wrinkle my nose.

He leaves my gaze to put the cake down and hand me a fork. "I hope you like chocolate."

"I haven't had cake in over five years."

He frowns. "Really?"

I remember getting the first audition with Adrien, the agent I worked with at the time told me to lose ten pounds.

Adrien rolled his eyes, but for the next two months, I ran up and down Venice Beach, eating very little, and weighing myself daily. I never had issues with my weight, but I wanted to please. I wanted them to look at me and not question whether I would be good enough for the role. I had to be perfect.

"I'm an actress. I have an image I have to keep in the public eye." I shrug. "Fun fact, I'm also a vegan."

Silas laughs. "Why didn't you say anything?"

"You're already doing a lot for me, I wasn't going to make you cook me my special food," I add. "Plus, you make a killer spaghetti and meatballs."

"Antonio Belizzo's wife taught me how to make her sauce."

I guess he was very close with the family.

"It's really good," I say, grinning.

The fire cracks and pops, making me break eye contact with him to glance at the embers. This has got to be my favorite part of being in this town. The roaring flames that dance all night. They're calming and pretty to look at. We rarely have fires back home. And when we do, they're gas fires, not natural ones with logs and poker sticks. Ever roast a marshmallow over real flames from a burning log? It hits differently than gas-powered flames.

He smiles. "Thanks, Parker." Mmph, I love the way he says my name. Why did we have to meet under such fucked-up circumstances?

I take one of the forks and scoop a piece of cake out, holding it to his mouth. He grins, taking it off the fork and licking his lips. I take a bite for myself, my mouth is salivating.

Whenever I have a sugary craving, I drink iced tea or yogurt. My birthday cakes were usually sugar-free, gluten-free, and vegan. Disgusting right? Well, being an actress makes you do stupid shit to stay on top.

The cake touches my tongue and I moan softly, going in for a second bite before offering Silas more. He shoots back the rum, then accepts my offering. God, watching the fork slide out of his mouth is a throb all on its own, I have to cross my legs.

I take another bite for myself. "Hope you don't mind sharing a fork."

"I already gave you mouth-to-mouth," he says, pouring more rum into his glass and adding more to mine even though I didn't take any yet.

And here I am wondering what that would feel like. The alcohol has finally hit me.

I giggle. "And saw me naked?"

"Not by choice, you were left for dead like that."

I uncross my legs and hike the t-shirt up a little. It's getting hot in here all of a sudden. "How did you warm me up?" I gulp some rum and grimace.

He scratches at his upper arm and grins. "Took you in a hot bath, then held you until you woke up."

Great, now I'm imagining us taking a bath together.

"Ah, much like you did last night?"

"Mm," he responds, shooting his rum back.

There's a tingle in the pit of my stomach that's moving lower. I don't want it to, but I can't help it. The growl in his voice when he's tired like tonight does it for me. His fucking face does it for me. Add alcohol to the mix, and that does it for me. I might have to sit on his face tonight to suppress this tingle. Ouff, I need a session with my therapist.

I get very sexual very fast when I drink, and Adrien loves it. Yet here I am doing my flirty drunk technique on Silas. What's wrong with you, Parker? "I'll have you know, these aren't real." I chuckle. "A gift from my dear old husband when my name became known."

"Never would've noticed," he says, sipping his drink. "I was too busy trying to save you from hypothermia to give them a good look."

I laugh at this because it sounds oddly gentlemanly of him. I wonder what he's like as a lover, what he's like as a father, and just as a friend. He isn't intimidating to me anymore, although he has this stare that seeps deep into your soul. As if he can tell what I'm thinking and what I want from a single look. I like looking at him for some reason. Mind you, I probably am only attracted to him because of all the fucked-up shit that's happening to me recently. Whenever something bothers me or I need a moment of release, I screw Adrien until he cries and begs for me to stop. I love being in control in the bedroom. It is definitely my strong suit. And right now, I need a distraction.

I take another bite of the cake and offer more to Silas. He takes it without question. His lips slide on the fork as he pulls away. A bit of icing kisses the middle of his lips before he licks it away. Ouff, you're killing me, Silas.

"So tell me," I start, putting the fork down and curling my leg up onto the couch to face him. "What do you do around here for fun?"

"Get really drunk and smoke some pot," he jokes, lifting the rum to my lips.

"You don't miss the city life at all?"

"Not as much as you'd think. I was never home when I worked, and when I was, I wasn't really there. So when we spoke about moving here, I felt like we could finally be a family. But she never liked it here. She never liked a lot of the things we did, having Jack included. Only married me so she didn't have to work as a part-time paralegal anymore and I could pay for all her shit. Moving here would've been good for my boy and me. She wasn't happy, but we were. And seeing him smile was all that mattered."

I don't want to tell him about the photo I found in the room I sleep in. A photo he probably put there. "He must've been cute."

"Mm," he says, throwing back the rest of his rum and looking at me. I'm not sure if it's because he wants me to do the same, so I do.

Exhaling sharply, Silas opens a little drawer in the coffee table and pulls out a purposely rusted framed photo of his son. He isn't smiling in the photo, his lips are slightly quirked up. Water droplets cover his face and those eyes of his shine brightly on that sunny day. He was a cute kid, and it breaks my heart that I have to see his face knowing what happened to him. Knowing that there's nothing Silas can do to change any of it.

"He's a real cutie," I comment, keeping a smile on my face.

"Yeah, he was a little firecracker."

I study the picture a little more, looking at him before speaking. "Did you guys ever plan on having more?"

"I wanted more, but she was dead set against it. Said Jackie ruined her body enough, she would never do it again."

I can see a pang of annoyance on his face. It's clear this was a constant argument between the two.

I really don't know what else to say. "I'm sure having a baby does put a strain on the body. Especially someone like you said your wife is. Y'know, obsessed with her figure."

"Ex-wife," he corrects again.

I nod. "Sorry, yeah."

He nods, too, and looks into the fire. I always found it so mesmerizing. The way the fire dances around, the orange embers aching from the heat. We used to go camping, my brother and I, with our neighbors the Jones'. At first, my mother didn't mind it. They had a son my brother's age and a daughter a couple of years old than I was. When their daughter started dating, however, our camping days were over. The last thing my mother wanted was for Chalice's sluttiness to rub off on me. I mean, it kind of did. Not even a year later I was screwing Jed at the church we attended every Sunday. But my mother didn't need to know that. Being in this town and this cabin reminds me a lot of those summers camping. I miss it.

"How do you like the cake?" he asks, getting up and pouring more rum into our glasses before adding a few logs to the dying fire. It jolts to life, emanating heat, which I don't mind. It's freezing tonight.

"It's good." I glance behind me at the boarded-up window and the darkness seeping in from the other one. My eyes are playing tricks on me again. I see a man standing in the window, just at the cusp of the reflecting light. His boots poke out onto the snow and my heart starts beating quickly. Did he find me or am I just getting really drunk that I'm seeing things?

Silas sits back down, closer to me this time. "I wasn't sure what flavor you liked. But you can never go wrong with chocolate."

I take a shuddered breath and give Silas a meek smile before looking back out the window. There's no one out there.

My breath grows short and shallow, and my palms get clammy. "Chocolate's always the answer." There's evident fear in my tone. Adrien's coming back for me. It's only a matter of time.

Silas raises his eyebrows at me as he gulps from his drink. "You okay?"

I point at the window, inhaling sharply. "I thought I saw someone."

He jumps from his seat and takes the bat from beside the stairs. A light flicks on. There's no one outside the window. Yep, I'm drunk. So drunk I'm seeing things.

He opens the door and looks out. "Ain't no one here."

I sigh, placing my hand on my head. "Sorry."

He locks the door and leaves the light on so I can see that no one is out there. "It's all right."

I gulp more rum. "Doesn't it freak you out being by yourself out here?"

"At first it did. I was so used to the loudness of the city, and the quiet out here is a lot. Sometimes I think I'm hearing things but it's just my paranoia kicking in."

I nod in agreement, staring out the window again. "The longer I look out the window it's like I can see people standing outside."

"Mm," he mumbles and chuckles softly. "Could be a wolf or a moose. We get those around here quite often. Don't think bears are out of hibernation yet to be poking around. Some can be, though."

"Or deranged assholes like my husband looking for me and making sure I'm really dead," I spit out, swearing I can see him standing in the darkness again, a puff of smoke leaving his lips. I hate it when he smokes. The nasty taste on his tongue always lingers too long and makes me gag. He doesn't smoke often, only when he plays poker with his buddies or has business meetings I'm not allowed to attend. It's disgusting, but I have no say over something that he rarely does.

"He ain't gonna come by here again any time soon. If he's asking around and breaking into people's houses along the river, then he's got at least ten homes to get to before he whips back around to mine." Silas clears his throat and gulps his drink, pushing mine to my lips.

Why is he trying to get me drunk? Well, trying is an understatement. I'm already there.

A creak moves through the house, bouncing off the walls before I shoot my attention to the upper floor. I listen intently, but the howling winds outside make it hard to know where the creak comes from. Can Adrien be in the house? Did he never even leave? Jesus, fuck.

"No one can get in here aside from that door, right?" I ask, my nerves on overdrive.

He licks his lips. "You don't have to worry."

"They got in here once, who says they can't do it again?" A scoff leaves my lips at how petty he thinks I'm being. I'm fucking scared, let me be scared.

"Well, I've added another latch to the front door, and I doubt they'll be so stupid as to break the second window knowing I fixed the first. And if Adrien is as smart as he seems, he'd have looked up the owners of the homes he's invading and he would've discovered who I am and who I'm affiliated with. You're safe, Parker, I promise," he assures. Yet I'm still on edge, even in my state.

"Maybe if I drink some more, then I won't have this nerve-wracking fear that he'll pop into the house," I say, pouring more rum into my glass even though it isn't empty.

He shoots back what's left in his glass and holds it out to me. "Top me off."

I let out a rush of air and remind myself that it's my birthday, the one day out of the year I'm allowed to be selfish and think of myself. Not worry about my husband. The fear and wonder can wait until tomorrow.

I nod, even though Silas doesn't say anything, and allow myself to drink until I pass out. I deserve it. "I'm not gonna lie." I giggle. "I'm really feeling it."

"I'm getting there," he adds, clinking my glass.

I take another gulp, grimacing. A chill sweeps up my spine, and I can't shake it off. There's something outside, I know there is, and they're creeping their way into the house. Roaming. Waiting. Watching. Just aching for a chance to get me. Why me? I don't understand what I did to deserve this shit. Then again, I did sleep my way to the top. Didn't I? Yes, it was with one person who became my husband before my fame struck hard. Or was it because I ran away from home and stole money from a church? This is karma getting back at me for doing things the wrong way. The sex was great at least.

Something rattles in the distance. A scraping sound follows with a crash of metal on the ground. We turn our attention to it and all I think about is the boarded windows. Someone is trying to get in.

Silas shoots the rest of his drink back and quietly sets it down, looking around the back of the house for some form of movement. My hands are already shaking when I finish off my drink and move closer to him. I swear I can feel a hand touch my shoulder but no one is there.

The second he rises, I'm on my feet, following him as he pulls a silver-colored gun from the side of the couch cushion. How many damn guns are in this house?

My hand slithers its way into his and he gawks at me before he holds it back. Why do I have to be tipsy right now?

We walk toward the rustling and banging of metal on metal. My heart is beating in my ears so loudly. There's another bang, it's coming from the door at the back—why didn't he tell me about the back door? It's a partial wooden door and a partial glass door. This one isn't boarded up. Maybe because the window is higher? There's a yellow light casting a glow onto the white snow. It doesn't look like snow at all, though. Not with the light shining on it. The snow appears disturbed, not necessarily footprints disturbing it, but something definitely has.

The bang clangs again and he peers out the window, looking side to side, then sighs and chuckles. It's a small family of raccoons trying to get into the garbage cans at the back of the house, their grunts echo the silent night.

"Fuck, it's too damn quiet here," I say, leaning back against the wall and letting go of his hand.

"You get used to it after a while." He opens the door and picks up a wooden board, hanging it on little hooks above the window. Guess he forgot to board this one just like he forgot to tell me there was a back door. Then again, I should've just assumed.

"You really like the seclusion out here?"

He tucks the gun into the back of his jeans. "I do."

He gives me a once-over, my erect nipples making themselves known in the t-shirt I'm sporting. I'm wearing nothing but this again. Just his shirt and nothing else. It's weird how comfortable I am around him. We lock eyes and I don't know if it was the thrill of the moment, the fright boiling within me, my drunken ass, or the fact that he keeps looking at my tits, but I grab his neck and pull it toward me, kissing him hungrily. He reciprocates and pushes me into the wall, lifting me against it with a grunt. He's a little rusty, but that's okay. I take the lead because I want this kiss badly.

The heat of the moment dies down as soon as another clang shakes the door. I move away from him, realizing I shouldn't do this. I'm still married and he's a broken man who hasn't been with someone in six years. It's enough that people see us together in town, the last thing I need is another scandal.

He leans forward to kiss me again but I push my lips together and move away. "I'm sorry, I didn't mean to do that," I say softly.

"It's okay." He leans forward again but as his lips touch mine, I quickly turn my head away.

"I think I've had too much to drink."

He puts me down. "Okay."

I start walking away from him toward the staircase. "I'll, um, thank you for dinner and cake. It was really nice of you. I-I'll see you in the morning."

"Yeah. Happy birthday, Parker," he calls out before I jog up the stairs and hear a heavy sigh.

Why did I do that? Fuck, sometimes my inner, horny self takes over and she doesn't know what to do with herself. Sex is like a drug to me. Always has been from the ripe age of fifteen. The second I see an attractive person, my insides go wild. When I first laid eyes on Silas, I was a goner. I need the release to function. Probably why Adrien and I screw so much. My therapist is right, I am a sex addict.

I'll never forget last year when Adrien and I screwed during a conference call. No one knew, but by God was it hard to stay quiet—I love when he pounds me against his desk—the windows surrounding us provide a free show to anyone who's watching. Or when I get on all fours in front of him while he tries to work and force him to eat me out. Mmph, I love when we're spontaneous like that. Looking back, it appears as if he loved me and found me irresistible, but now, I'm not sure at all.

CHAPTER 13

Morning comes much quicker than I thought it would and I hear Silas banging and clanging dishes. I'm sure he doesn't mean to be as loud as he is, given he's been living alone for six years, but I'd appreciate the silence. My head is pounding up a storm.

I quietly tiptoe to the washroom and prepare myself for the day. No idea what will be in store for me now, hopefully, a reply back from someone. I'm hoping I still know my brother. When we were kids, he wasn't the type to betray me. We were always close. When he had a bad dream, it was my room he ran to. When he got hurt, he called for me, not Mom or Dad. But he could still be mad at me for leaving. Please don't be mad at me, Jacks.

I find pain relievers in the washroom and pop two tablets to calm my headache. Nothing like a hangover the day after my birthday. Adrien always leaves two tablets with a glass of water the day after my birthday. I always party too hard this time of year.

I make my way back to my room to find Silas walking up the stairs holding my clothes neatly folded in his arms. He washed them the other night for me. Another thing he did without me asking. I appreciate this man so much.

"Morning," he says, giving me a grin.

"Hi."

He looks me up and down, trying to avoid eye contact, but catches my eyes for a fraction of a second. Ouff, I can cut the tension with a knife over here. "I had to switch mine over, so..." He hands me the pile of clothing.

I take the clothes and stand there for a moment, nibbling my bottom lip. It's evident there's this sexual tension building up from our kiss last night, which neither of us can express. It was out of character for me, too. I'm not a cheat, nor have I ever wanted to. But with everything going down the past week, betrayal seems like something my husband deserves.

But goddammit, do I need a fix. The kiss was all my urges spewing out of me from this pent-up lust toward my savior.

Silas looks behind him and tongues his cheek before scratching the back of his head. "I'm gonna make breakfast. Come down when you're ready."

I nod. "Yeah, of course."

Of course? Who am I talking to? My doctor? I never say of course unless I'm talking to a professional.

He starts down the stairs, but before I can even see him leave, I'm already in my room putting the clothes on the bed. I let out a sigh and groan. Damn, I need something to tame this rage screaming between my thighs. I seriously wish there was a lock on this door right now. I hate being in the mood alone. The number of times I've screwed Adrien when he didn't want it or wasn't in the mood is astounding. I'd make him fuck me by pissing him off so he'd need a release.

This moment here is no different. The only difference is, I don't have Adrien because he tried to kill me. But I have Silas, and he's been nothing but nice to me. It seems only natural to return the favor like this since I don't have access to my accounts. Doesn't it? God, I'm twisted sometimes—mind you, I'm just horny. Sorry, Adrien, but I think the guilt I should be feeling for cheating on you is long gone. You tried to kill me. That merits doing whatever the fuck I want.

Silas' footfalls move quickly up the stairs. Shit, maybe there's someone outside. Oh, God, please tell me we're safe. The door bursts open and Silas walks in, grabbing my face and kissing me passionately. Our tongues do a sweep, sliding, roaming, and flicking. He's kissing me like his life depended on it.

I back away for a breath of air, those jade eyes glazing over. Well, I guess I'm getting what I wan after all.

It doesn't take long for our clothes to disappear. His rugged breathing caresses my face as he lifts me. He lets out a few grunts, lying us on the bed and I have to say, it is doing it for me. It's a raging waterfall down there.

It feels weird to have someone who isn't Adrien on top of me, but right now, Adrien can go fuck himself and the white horse he rode in on.

Silas kisses my neck, then trails his kisses to my lips again. I take the lead and swirl my tongue in his mouth. He's still rusty, but I don't care. I need a good dicking. I hope he's good at this.

"I don't have a condom," he says, staring into my eyes even though my perfect tits are on display.

I groan. "Shit." Guess this isn't happening.

"Is it okay if I pull out?"

Mmph, even lying naked on top of me with his dick erect against my leg he's a gentleman.

"I really don't care what you do, I just want you to fuck me right now."

A grin touches his lips and he pushes himself into me on the third try. He's a lot bigger than Adrien, and I can certainly tell the difference. Silas starts rocking, slowly at first, like he's trying to find a good rhythm. But after a few minutes, I'm starting to get bored. He isn't even pressed against me. It makes me think he doesn't want to do this. His hands are in fists on either side of me and he's lifted, the only part of us touching is what's connecting us right now. What irks me, even more, is he won't grab my tits. Do something! Bite me, lick them, suckle them, kiss me. Am I that sadistic I can't even make love anymore?

I grab his neck and pull his face to mine, pushing him onto his back so I can take control. Our lips part and I ride him as rough as I want. No scratch that, like I need. He seems so much bigger now, but the pain is exhilarating. Finally, he grabs my tits, and a growl rumbles through him. It's evident he hasn't done this in a while. Don't worry. I got this, baby.

Being the controlling one in the relationship is always my favorite, although when Adrien takes charge and slams me against whatever piece of furniture we have, I fucking love it. We're lucky nothing ever broke. Adrien and I are pretty reckless when we're in the heat of the moment. We've broken our fair share of bed frames, tables, chairs, and a desk once.

Silas turns me over, shoving himself back inside me and taking me savagely like I want. He pounds me, moving our bodies higher up the bed until my head hits the headboard. I put my palms onto it, feeling him thrust deeply into me as I scream out in pleasure. It's been a while since I've been screwed like this.

"Fuck," he says through gritted teeth as I bite down on his neck.

"Oh, yes, Silas!" I roll my head back. "Right there!"

He thumps harder, hurting me but it feels so damn good. Just as his lips touch mine and I feel him ready to pull out and cum on me, one of the legs on the bed breaks, nearly sending us into the side table. I let out a yelp and grab onto him as he holds onto the headboard to stop us from barrelling off the bed.

"Shit," he says out of breath.

We look beside us, out of breath and satisfied, before making eye contact.

I laugh. "You know the sex is good when stuff breaks."

"Are you okay?"

"Yeah," I reply, letting out a sigh of satisfaction.

He grunts, adjusting his grip on me. "I finished inside you."

"We'll take a trip to the pharmacy." I kiss him softly, meeting his eyes. "A little unexpected."

"Extremely." He rolls off me but pulls me close so we're lying on the opposite side of the bed. "Sorry for being a little out of place."

I turn on my side to face him. "That's why I went on top."

I'm trying to catch my breath and hide my shy smile. He stares at me as if star-struck. I'm never this easy—then again, it didn't take Adrien long to sleep with me, Jed, either. The few other guys I fooled around with only had to get me drunk...maybe I am a floozy? What's Adrien going to think of me when he finds out about this? You now what? Fuck him. He's screwing some French bitch, isn't he?

Silas moves hair off my shoulder and tucks a few strands behind my ear. He's so fucking sexy, it's hard to look away, especially naked. He's got such a great body and that dick. Goddamn.

His fingers slide down my jawline and teeter off my chin, falling delicately onto my arm that's propping me up on the bed and giving me gorgeous cleavage. He doesn't look at my tits, he looks into my eyes. He's so beautiful. How did I get so lucky to have a savior as handsome as him?

His thumb brushes my arm and he smiles softly. "Now I don't want you to leave."

I chuckle, biting my bottom lip. "I'm not annoying you yet?"

He lets out a breath, licking those lips in the fashion he does when I say something he doesn't like. "No."

I stick my tongue between my teeth. "Liar."

I wonder if he'd think I was unsatisfied if I ask him to go again? "Mm, I needed that."

He laughs, getting comfortable on his stomach and resting his head on his fists. "You're really good at it."

I laugh, shimmying my shoulders. "Why thank you."

"Get around as a celebrity?"

I click my tongue. "I'm not a whore, if that's what you're asking."

"I wasn't," he says, eyeing my cleavage for a second.

I wipe my under my lip and meet his gaze. "I've been with Adrien for eight years, and a handful of guys before that."

I don't know why I want him to know, but I tell him about the guys I was with. They're nothing to run home about. A couple of them were extras, and one of them is also a major star. Samuel Withers. We had one night together a week before I met Adrien. Sam and I don't talk about that night. We were sad and desperate and a little intoxicated. It was sloppy sex in the closet of a resto-bar. We nod at each other at events, but nothing more than that. I'm not embarrassed by him, but if word got out, the last thing we need is a scandal. Celebrity magazines and news channels ache for something juicy they can sink their teeth in. The night Sam and I got together sure is a juicy one. Adrien doesn't even know about that encounter, and I tell him everything.

Silas places his hand on mine, slithering our fingers together. "How is it being a celebrity?"

I sputter and shake my head. "I mean, it has its quirks and its annoyances. I never have privacy for one. Can't go anywhere without someone stopping you for an autograph or a photo. Sometimes I just want to eat dinner or do groceries without someone sniffing down my neck." I shrug. "I think this is the first time since I became famous that I don't have to worry about paparazzi being in my yard."

"You're always welcome to stay, Parker." He grins. "For as long as you need to."

"Thanks, Silas." I truly appreciate his generosity. "I can't believe we've only known each other for a week. I feel like I've known you my whole life but also don't know anything about you."

"I'm an open book." His lips quirked up into a smile. "Ask away."

I chuckle nasally and bite my lower lip. There's so much I want to know about him and there's also so much I want to do to him. I doubt he'll be able to go again...I can't help but want to sit on his face. His lingering stare is far too much for my self-control. Focus, Parker. My mind is drawing a blank. I need food in my system, some coffee, too. Then I'l ask away.

I get up and take the wool sweater he always wears and drape it over my naked body. "I'm wearing this until we gotta leave."

"I already told you I like it when you wear my clothes." He follows suit getting into his cotton boxers. Adrien loves wearing boxers with bizarre patterns every day of the week. I wear them sometimes around the house. They're big on me but still look cute.

I hop down the stairs and enter the kitchen. Silas was about to start making something by the array of food on the counter. "What's for breakfast?"

He pulls on a crisp white t-shirt, joining me in the kitchen. "What're you feeling?" He pushes me into the counter.

I giggle as he suckles my neck and turns me around. I love kitchen sex. I'm lifted onto the counter and right as I feel the release from our last go leak out of me, there's rapping on the door. Aggressive at that. A grunt leaves him and he steps away from me, leaving me on the counter with my legs open for the world to see my business. Did he seriously just abandon me like this?

The rapping commences again and he looks out the window. An aggravated breath escapes his mouth. Great, now someone is going to interrupt my fun in this frozen hellhole.

As soon as the door opens, the cold sweeps in and fills the kitchen. "Lou, what the fuck are you doing here?" Silas says, shock and embarrassment in his tone. This must be the famous Louisa.

She rubs her growing baby bump that doesn't fit into her jacket. "Did Anne not give you my messages? I told you the first Saturday of January I'd be here to pick up some of Jackie's things."

"Yeah, yeah, I got your messages." He turns to me as I hop off the counter. "I forgot."

She glances behind her as a man gets out of a van in Silas' front yard. "Can I come in?"

"Sure," Silas answers, opening the door wider. I instinctually put on the sunglasses and fold my arms from the cold and the fact that I'm not wearing anything aside from his wool sweater, which doesn't leave much to the imagination.

"Oh, hi?" Lou looks at me and scowls at Silas as if he isn't allowed to have company.

His ex-wife is here. Yikes. She looks very different in person than she does in the one photo I saw of her. Her hair is pulled back in a short, tight ponytail, and she has highlights. She's pregnant again, and I can't help but wonder how Silas feels about this. He said she never wanted more kids. Perhaps just not with him. I guess it's true that she didn't love him at all.

"Louisa, this is my, um..." Silas gives me a shrug.

"Parker," I say, remaining where I am. Shit, I shouldn't have said my actual name. This bitch looks crazy. She has this scowling look about her. If looks could kill, Louisa would have shot me and Silas dead by now. The last thing I want to do is stir some shit. Until my shit is resolved, I don't want more shit stirred.

She points between the two of us. "So you two are...?"

Silas shrugs again. "Yes."

"Something like that?" I chuckle awkwardly. "I'm making breakfast, are you joining us?"

"No, I'm just here to pick up some of my things." She glares at Silas. "Help me upstairs?"

He glances at me. "Yeah." Then charges upstairs with Louisa following after.

As much as I hate the drama in my life, I'm addicted to the juice and listen closely while taking the things from the counter to continue making the western omelet he started.

"I didn't know you were seeing someone," Louisa says, stepping into their son's room.

"We don't talk."

"You could've called me back when Anne gave you my messages."

"After Jack died, you left in the middle of the night without a note. Emptied half the bank account, and then a week later I get them divorce papers in the mail with the deed to this house in my name. As far as I know, we were over well before you up and left." He moves some boxes around. His accent lightens up a bit, but I pay no mind to it.

Louisa takes a breath. "I want the baby clothes."

"That all you're taking?"

"I was wondering if I could take it all? We're having a boy, and I want little Noah to be able to play with his brother's things."

"You can take everything but this one." He grunts and drops a box. "And whatever is in the closet."

"Okay." She clears her throat. "Is it all right if my husband comes in? It'll be easier to move everything."

"Yeah, whatever." I watch Silas disappear into the room I'm sleeping in to get his pants on.

Louisa starts down the stairs with a box marked Stuffed Animals in hand as he matches into Jack's room again. Silas doesn't seem too happy.

I stop cutting up peppers and go upstairs as well, I can't really stand here half-naked any longer. I disappear into the room and clothe myself in the once neatly folded laundry that's now scattered on the floor. As bad as I should feel for Silas, the one sick and twisted thought that runs through my head is that he's going to need me to release some of the annoyance and anger building up, and I can't fucking wait. Yes, I get it. I'm fucked in the head. It's no wonder my husband wanted to have me killed.

"Brian?" Louisa calls from the doorway. "There's boxes to carry, c'mon."

I'm fixing Silas' Harvard sweater over my petite body and am met by him carrying two boxes labeled Toys to the stairs. "Hey, you want me to help?"

"No," he replies coldly. "Just stay outta the way."

Okay? Calm your fucking tits.

I put my hands up and slide my feet into a pair of socks, going back to the kitchen to continue doing what I was doing. "Jeez."

Brian walks in, he's the complete opposite of Silas. Bright blond hair, dark brown eyes, no beard, a little overweight, and seems as useless as they come. He slips out of his boots and looks at me. Why are you looking at me? It's not my house.

I sigh and point up the stairs when Silas follows after him.

"I'm Brian, it's nice to meet you," Brian says, putting his hand out to Silas at the top of the stairs.

"Mm," Silas grunts. It must be really hard to go through your dead son's things with your ex-wife and her new husband, but at least say hi to the man. "All the boxes in this room, just not the ones in the closet. Or anything in the closet."

Brian nods. "Cool."

Silas comes back down the stairs, placing boxes by the door and getting into his boots. Louisa makes her way past him and sits at the dining table, slightly out of breath. There's this quirk about her that's admiring. She has this aura of fun and spontaneity. And she's a unique kind of beautiful. She looks like a bitch, but a fun bitch I'd want to be friends with under different circumstances. I can understand what Silas saw in her all those years ago, how he tried to love her when she got pregnant and make them a family. She didn't seem happy, even now, though.

"Would you like something to drink?" I ask, cracking a few eggs into a bowl.

"No, thanks." She looks up at Silas as he kicks his boots off and moves by Brian to get more boxes. "Where'd you meet Silas?"

How can she look at Silas with such disgust in her eyes? He's gorgeous. They had a son together. There's history between them. Messy history, but history all the same. Mind you, I love Adrien with everything that I am, yet I think I'd look at him in the same manner if he were in front of me right now. Disgust and loathing.

I have no idea how to even put into words what my relationship with Silas is. At least not yet. "We kinda just popped into each other's lives recently."

The thought of leaving Adrien never once crossed my mind. He's a jealous fuck who hates me even looking at another man that I'm not working with. I never have to worry about him, either. He's the best-looking producer in Hollywood, but his eyes are only for me. Aside from a couple of suspicious women who try to claw their way into our bed, my mind never once thought of him as a cheater. Yet here I am, being that cheater.

"You're not his type," Louisa spits out as he's making his way to the door again.

Silas scoffs. "And you'd know what my type is?"

"It's definitely not someone who leaves bite marks all over your neck," Louisa snaps.

I do agree, hickies are kind of a childish thing to do. But goddamn the sex we just had was intense. If I wasn't biting on his neck, I'd have bit my lip to blood.

"You left me remember, not the other way around so stop acting like the victim and making it look like it's my fault," he roars, jamming his feet into his boots as Brian slowly puts his on.

Brian and I are on the sidelines just taking this in and seeing how far they can go and how loud they can get. I wonder if Silas has any popcorn.

Louisa glares at me for a response. "How old are you any-way?"

Why am I dragged into this? "I'm twenty-seven."

Louisa shrieks. "She's eight years younger than you. What are you doing, Silas?"

This bitch has some fucking nerve.

"My God, what does it matter? You're too old to be having another kid, you don't hear me whining about it." Silas takes his boots off again and disappears upstairs.

If I can comment "L.O.L." on this whole argument, I would. Seriously, though, where are we on the popcorn?

"You need to calm down, babe," Brian says softly.

Louisa sputters and lets out a rush of air through her flaring nostrils. "I can't calm down in this fucking house. Every time I see his face all I see is Jackie."

Brian squeezes her shoulders, massaging gently. "Then why don't you wait in the car? Close your eyes and do your breathing techniques."

This bitch must have an anger problem.

I push the sunglasses up my nose and look over at her as she scowls me in the sweater that belongs to Silas. I struck a nerve I didn't want to strike. I'm cold, that's why I put this on.

"Why do you look so familiar?" she asks, her tone calmer and curious.

"Just have one of those faces." I nod, spotting Silas drop boxes on the floor, and go back upstairs for more.

She's definitely the last person I want to ask for help. I'm waiting on my brother. He's going to know what to do. I have to trust that he will.

"Did you hear what happened to that actress around here?" She looks at Silas who drops the last of the boxes on the floor for Brian to bring to the car.

"Heard they found her body by the Kroger's," Silas says, coming over to me and turning on the stove. His hand rests gently on my lower back.

She watches us like she's about to pounce on us. A predator watching its prey. "You hear anything from the house they rented?"

He groans quietly, annoyed at her being here. 'House is on the other side of the river, can't hear much from over here." He squeezes my shoulder before starting a pot of coffee.

Would it be so bad if she recognized me? Another set of helping hands might be a good thing. But when she gives me another once-over and scoffs, making a disgruntled face. My quest for help takes a standstill when it comes to this woman.

She looks over at Brian and notices the boarded-up window. "What happened to the window?"

"Couple of wolves have been roaming around these parts. Marlow lost her shit one night and ran into the window." Silas leaves a soft kiss on my head. "She's at Marty's for a few days."

Oh, that sets her off. She looks like she's snarling like a dog. "And how long are you staying here?"

Why is any of this any of your business?

I sigh. "No idea."

She reminds me of a co-star I worked with a few years ago for a film called "Deviation". Charlie Ferdinando. Typical white chick with too much money to spend and one too many Botox treatments. But we worked well off each other on-screen. Our acting chemistry was fire. Then as soon as the cameras stopped filming, there she was again, that little witch who knew she could get what she wanted if she wrapped her fat, injected lips onto someone's cock. Even though she was a great actress, she only got as famous as she did because of the long list of blows her name was attached to.

Brian wipes his boots on the welcome mat. "All packed.'

"Great," Louisa says, pushing herself up with the table for support. "I'll just give it a run-through and take a few of my things out of the guest room I left behind."

Oh shit, well, she'll definitely see the mess in that room that still smells like sex. Wonder what she'll say about that.

Brian rolls back and forth from the balls of his feet to his toes and clasps his hands behind him. He's as uncomfortable as I am to watch this dead relationship try and communicate like normal human beings.

"You guys driving home?" Silas asks Brian, setting the table for us.

"Yep, making our way through Canada to Connecticut." He stands firmly on his feet. "There's actually a couple boxes in the van that are yours. Before I forget...where should I leave them?"

Silas waves a hand by the bookshelf near the door. "Anywhere is fine."

Louisa starts making her way back to us. "What happened in the spare room? It's a mess in there." Louisa slowly walks down the stairs with a couple of things in her arms.

Silas flashes me a grin. "Moving some stuff around."

The way his cheeks flush makes me smile, too. My knees want to buckle under me just thinking of the last moments before the bed broke. Unlike anything I've had with any man.

"The bed is broken." She points out. "That was my mother's."

He chuckles, looking at me again. "Easy fix."

Make it obvious that we broke it why don't you?

Yes, make it obvious. I want her to know that Silas is happy again. After six fucking years, there isn't an aura of sadness consuming him.

She constantly looks at me in this fashion as if she doesn't know if she can see clearly or not. If she squints anymore, she'll pop the veins bulging on her forehead. Demonic-looking little fucker. "Did you guys have sex on that bed?"

Silas scoffs, sliding a hand to my shoulder. "Don't see how that's any of your concern."

She lets out a little growl. "It's mine and it's broken."

"Then yes, we fucked in that bed," Silas answers, rolling his eyes. "What does it fucking matter? I'll fix it when I get a chance."

She drops her things on the table. "God, you're unbelievable." Then puts her fists on her hips.

The demonic little fucker on her forehead has a twin in her neck. It's pulsating and bulging with every grit of her teeth and every gulp she takes. As much as I want this to continue so I can sit back and watch this reality show, she's also pregnant. Stress cannot be good for the baby.

Brian steps forward, taking her hand. "Babe, come now, you have to relax."

"Ugh, whatever," she says, strutting for the door.

An aggravated breath leaves Silas. "I'd say it was nice to see you, but..." He shrugs.

"Nice to meet you both," Brian says, trying to ease the tension.

Nothing can ease this tension. I wonder if they were always like this. Hate-fucked each other until an accident happened and they chose to see where their relationship would go. I can't imagine what that must be like. Forced to be with someone so that your child can seemingly live in a happy family. When in reality, it isn't. Silas deserves the world, and this bitch is doing nothing but crumbling all the years of hurt he went through.

Louisa stops, turning to me, and narrows her eyes. "Kinda a coincidence you and that actress have the same name, isn't it?"

Well, if she didn't confirm she recognized me, this surely does. But if she recognized me, why isn't she gasping with shock? The headlines say you're dead, yet here you are, blah, blah, blah. I really don't like Louisa. She's rude and spiteful. Silas can do what he wants with his life, yet it's like he's not allowed to do anything and has to wallow in pity until the day he dies.

I roll my eyes. "I'm sure there is more than one Louisa in the world, hmm?"

She scoffs, rubbing her belly softly before looking up at me again. "He's a man of many secrets. Be careful. I left him, yes, but not because of Jackie," she says, leaving before I can ask her what she means.

What?

I whip my head at Silas and furrow my brows. What in the hell does she mean? Maybe the skeletons in his closet need to make themselves known. I never wanted to know any of Adrien's dark side of the business, but parts of me are always curious. Much like I am right now. I don't want to know anything, but I need to know everything.

"Such a manipulative—mm," Silas grunts, slamming drawers shut.

"Hey?" I say softly, giving Brian a grin as he pushes the boxes with his foot to close the door. We're left in silence for a moment. The wave of awkwardness slowly leaves and is replaced by rage.

He slams more drawers, tossing things around the kitchen. His fists are clenched and he's huffing as he stares out the window, watching Louisa drive off. I can't imagine what's going on in his head. Especially seeing her pregnant again.

He snags the bag of bread off the counter and stands beside me again, staring at the toaster. His face is still flush, and the veins in his neck are bulging. He's pissed.

"It's okay, Silas. She's gone."

He clears his throat and pops some bread into the toaster. "I forgot she was coming."

A short laugh leaves me. "She seems nice."

"She's a real bitch. Only stayed with her because of Jackie hoping it would turn into something more."

I rub my hand up and down his back, watching the bulging veins relax as I remove the sunglasses. "Why didn't she just get an abortion?"

He meets my eyes. "She's...I guess I can say, against it. I thought we could make it work because of all the flirting and sex. Boy, was I wrong."

There it is again. That sadness. It came back just thinking of Louisa and how he tried to make them a family because of Jack. I want that sadness to go away and that smile to spread onto his lips like it was a few moments ago. He's beautiful when he smiles. Silas deserves to smile all the time.

"I know how you feel. My ex before Adrien was purely sex, but I was too stupid to realize it until I saw him making out with one of our roommates. He tried to make it look like he was drunk and thought it was me. But I'm not that stupid, well, maybe I am since I tried to make us work another two months while he continued to fuck our roommate—whose room I might add was across from mine." I smooth out the back of his neck. "Guess you can say I'm an idiot when it comes to relationships because as much as I love Adrien and the sex is wild, he's definitely not who I thought he was."

"Mm," he says, taking the butter from the counter and smothering the toast with it.

We don't say much during breakfast. I feel like the buzz about our intimacy die down the moment Louisa came into the house. Fucking bitch ruining my fun. Then again, I can't blame her for reacting the way she did. Silas is hot as hell, and Brian, well, he's the typical thick middle-aged man who gets out of breath from the couch to the fridge. And if I'm comparing myself to Louisa, she doesn't stand a chance. Though, she and Silas did make a handsome little man.

*

After breakfast, Silas clears the table as I head upstairs to pick up the clothes that are scattered on the ground. I'm not sure what exactly she took, but it's nothing that Silas recently purchased for me. A couple of drawers are open on the dresser, and that family photo of the three of them is missing. Why would she take this? It's not like she likes Silas very much so I highly doubt it's for memories of him.

I expected the day to come when Adrien cheated on me. It's easy for him, too. He meets hundreds of actresses and other producers, any one of them can flirt their way into our bed. At least he did it after I "died"...at least I hope so.

The woman's voice on the phone when I initially called him sounded so familiar. Her Parisian French accent reminds me of our month-long vacation in France. We made love for hours, nearly fourteen times in a day, then did nothing but drink coffee, and eat pastries. There isn't a time I look back on that I regret with Adrien. Maybe this new woman of his is our translator from that trip? I remember how much they flirted when they thought I wasn't listening. How she stared at him and always made sure to wear low-cut tops and short skirts. Fucking slut.

After I refold the clothes and stuff them in the drawers, I check out what happened to the bed for it to collapse so easily. I get to my hands and knees and look under the bed. There's an envelope with red writing on the front of it. My curiosity peaks and I reach for it, but of course, my arms are too short.

"Fuck," I say quietly.

I wonder what it could be. A steamy love letter I can masturbate to later, naked Polaroids of Silas' dick, or maybe it's something boring that I don't need to see.

I feel like I can trust Silas, I mean, I let him inside me for fuck's sake. But Louisa's words keep circling. He's a man of many secrets. Be careful. I left him, yes, but not because of Jackie. What's he hiding? Goddamn, how did my life become a mystery novel?

"Parker?" Silas sounds, making me hit my head on the side table.

"Jesus fucking Christ!" I yelp, rubbing the side of my noggin. "You scared the shit out of me." I sit back on my feet and look up at him.

He chuckles, putting his hand out to me. "You scare too easy."

"Don't be so fucking quiet," I say, taking his hand and rising to my feet.

We lock eyes for a moment as if reminiscing on what happened here this morning. What broke the bed, what caused those hickies, and what's making us hotter by the second.

This thumb grazes my knuckles. "Ready when you are." I never realized how rough and calloused his hands are. God, is it turning me on right now?

I wet my lips and nod quickly. "Yeah, g-good to go."

But we don't move. We hold our stare, fixing our fingers to weave together. There's this intensity in his gaze. He's smiling, but something is stopping him from giving in and showing me a softer side to the kindness he's shown. And the devilish side we experienced earlier.

Regardless, if he stares at me like this any longer I will rip his clothes off and suck his dick like I'm mad at it.

He looks at the bed, then back at me. "She didn't take anything of yours, did she?"

I shake my head, blinking twice. "I don't have anything, to begin with."

"Mm," he grunts, letting go of my hand and making his way to the car.

God, this man is driving me nuts. I want to swim in his thoughts, let them take over and devour me. There's not an ounce of guilt washing over me, either. I feel clear, and slightly relaxed, for the first time in a long time. I needed this so-called break. Now to get to the bottom of what the fuck happened to me.

CHAPTER 14

W e listen to country music on the drive to town. It's actually kind of relaxing. There is no awkwardness between us anymore, and what makes my cheeks blush is he hesitantly takes my hand in his and squeezes it as we approach the town.

I wasn't looking for this. Christ, a week ago I was getting ready for a New Year's Eve party. Now look at me. Presumably dead to the world, my husband tried to kill me, I haven't been on any social media in eight days, oh, and I've found myself a sexy country boy to play with. What could get better than this, am I right?

Well, there is the fact that all my belongings, my money, my fame—it's gone now. What do I have aside from Silas? He's good for me. Isn't he?

He's a man of many secrets. I hate fucking secrets. Adrien kept the business side of his industry a secret from me and that definitely came back to bite me in the ass. I questioned quite often why he never told me about what he did when he wasn't working on producing films. He always said the same thing; Don't worry about it, babe, it's nothing you need to know unless it involves you. Now show me those tits so I can finish off this contract...well, maybe I added that last thing, but he did say it to me once when he needed a distraction from a psychotic director.

As much as he's pissing me off, I'd be lying if I said I didn't miss the sex. We were wild. From the day we met, right up to the New Year's Eve party—he took me three times that day as if he knew something was going to happen. Once in the shower that morning, another bent over his desk where he ate me out from behind and then shoved his dick inside when it was his turn to cum, and the third time was in the pantry during my second glass of champagne at the party. Maybe the problem with our relationship was we never communicated when we should have. Instead, we tore each other's clothes off as a way to shut the other up. But there was love there, I'm sure of it.

"Is there even a pharmacy in this town?" I ask as Silas parks in front of the café.

He lets go of my hand to kill the engine, threading our fningers once more. "Yeah, it's beside Doreen's."

I nod, looking in front of us at the dark red and black café. It's out of place, but I like it. I can see something like this in L.A., all the influencers taking selfies, uploading shots of their coffees and unique "Karat Muffins". I miss home. The noise, the insanity, the waves crashing on the shore. It would be nice to have my life back without the stress of it all.

I clear my throat and sniff. Always sniffling from the coldness. "We should check to see if anyone wrote back and I can get my life back."

He snickers. "Don't like your life now?"

I lean my head back and grin, tempted to climb onto his lap and show him how good our life can be. "Keep fucking me the way you did and I don't think I'll go anywhere."

He kisses my knuckles and laughs. "We can't break more furniture, though. There won't be anything left in the house if we do."

I unclip my belt and wrinkle my nose. "And if I get my money back I'll buy you all new furniture so we can break it again."

I get out of the truck and slide the sunglasses on. It's not like they make any difference. The number of times I've been spotted out and about with sunglasses on and my hair hidden in a hoodie is astounding. People see me all over the place. They may not know me personally, but if they watch enough of my movies, interviews, and events, they can familiarize themselves to recognize me even in a disguise I assume is working. And these sunglasses do nothing to hide my face.

He fixes the sunglass on my face. "I keep forgetting you're famous." He holds my face, leaving me with a soft kiss in the cold. He says that yet he was so curious about it earlier.

I stick my tongue between my teeth. "Getting with a famous person isn't all it's cracked up to be, is it?"

He gropes me, pulling me closer to him. "The sex was pretty good."

I raise my eyebrows. "Pretty good?" If he thinks that was pretty good, wait until I unleash what I have in store for him. "Oh, baby, wait until we get home."

He smiles, releasing my bum, and kissing me softly again. "I like that." He taps my nose with his. "Home."

I can crumble in his arms right now.

Silas, Silas, Silas, what on earth are you doing to me?

I'm famous, married, and dead to the world. The last thing I wanted was this.

Yet here I am. In it, wondering what the fuck it is.

With a deep, chilling breath, I tap his chest and make my way into the café, waving at Anne as I do before going to the computers. Silas smirks, follows me in, and heads to the counter to order us a coffee.

Anne watches me for a moment before acknowledging him. "Morning, Silas," she says, taking two medium-sized cups. "You hear Louisa's in town for the day."

He looks back at me and grins. "Yeah, she stopped by the house for some of Jack's things."

She pours hot coffee into the cups and places them in front of him. "I'm meeting with her for lunch at Gillian's 'round one. You and your girl are more than welcome to join us."

He shakes his head with his lips set in a hard line. "Lou wasn't too keen on meeting my girl seeing that she's a few years younger and a buttload prettier." He takes the coffee cups and places a five-dollar bill on the counter. "We're gonna have to decline your invitation."

Being called his girl has a new meaning now. This whole thing just got a whole lot more interesting, didn't it?

Although now it's making me nervous. What if we don't get along? What if I'm just experiencing Stockholm syndrome and I don't really want to do this thing that's happening between us? We slept together one time, is there even an us at this point? I'm jumping to conclusions. Computer. Focus on the computer in front of you, Parker.

My heart sinks as soon as I open my emails. Aside from the designer ads and countless happy birthday emails from friends I haven't opened yet, there are two that strike me. One from my brother, Jack, and the other from Adrien with the subject line that reads, we need to talk.

My breath catches in my throat. What could Adrien want to talk about? Oh, sorry for trying to have you killed, my bad? No, fuck you, Adrien, and that high horse you're still riding. You're going down.

I open Jack's email and he just writes, give me one more week. Well, shit. I'm stuck in this frozen version of hell for another damn week. I sit back in the chair and let out a breath. Fuck, I hate depending on people. Probably why I'm so independent. But I have to trust my brother and put all my faith in him. Karma, don't come and bite me in the ass now. Please.

I look out the window beside me, something bright catching my eye. There's a car parked across the street, the sun glaring off of it and flashing into the café. The tinted windows, matte black exterior, large stainless-steel rims, and thick grill on the front of it. The car is back. Adrien has a big dick, but his taste in cars is so flashy, that you'd think he was compensating. The longer I stare at the car, I notice there's someone in the front seat. I can't see their face, but I see their hands gripping the steering wheel. Shit. Is that Adrien?

"Black, one sugar," Silas says, causing me to jump out of my skin. "You all right?"

"Ye-yeah, just peachy," I say through a breath and look back out at the car that's now pulling away.

He sits beside me. "You look kinda pale."

I turn to face him. "I think I've seen that car before." No, I don't think. I know I saw that car before. Our lunch date, I saw it here. "Doesn't it look familiar?"

"So many tourists drive in and out of this town." He sips his coffee. "Could be. Why?"

I point at the computer. The unread email is right under my index finger. "I think it's Adrien's."

Anger builds up on Silas' face, his cheeks reddening. "You're not going to talk to him." He stares at the email, his tongue moving along his bottom lip. "Do not reply to that email, Parker."

"Oh, I know." I nod quickly, taking the coffee and looking at it. "That's all I need is to meet up with him and he shoots me dead."

He looks back out, scanning the area for something. The way his jaw tightens, clenches, and flexes, he's worried about me. This man who I barely even know is worried something bad will happen to me.

But after a few minutes of making sure nothing suspicious is outside, his attention is back on the computer, taking the mouse and snooping through my emails. "Any luck with your brother?"

"Mhm, asked for one more week." I point at the email, then scrunch my nose. "Should I call my agent?" I spit out, knowing I won't do it because Adrien and she are close. There isn't a movie, commercial, or photo shoot that she books that isn't run past him beforehand. If I call her, then I'm sure she'll call and inform him of my whereabouts.

"Why haven't you done that already?"

I pinch the bridge of my nose. "Adrien introduced us."

I've been through two agents since being with Adrien. One was a joke and lasted maybe a month before Adrien fired him. Said he didn't like the way he looked at me. And then there was Gertrude Goldstein. She is the best. She knows the type of actress I am and keeps pushing me to do things out of my comfort zone. Including winning me that Oscar three years ago. I'm proud of it, yes, but I don't feel like I deserve it. I was the first choice on a list of three actresses who were better suited for the job than I was, but because I'm married to a Bailey, I was chosen first.

The film I won was an empowering story of a broken husband and wife trying to survive their relationship while the world was literally crumbling around them. The emotions I had to exude and the pain I had to channel just to make the screams and heartache realistic, took a toll on me. I stopped accepting scripts six months after filming. I needed a break because the things brought up for my character also came home with me and put a strain on Adrien and me. We took a trip after that, just the two of us to the Maldives for three weeks. We spoke, we fucked, and spoke some more. In the end, we came out stronger than we ever were and I came out with an Oscar and a pregnancy scare.

Of course, I wasn't pregnant, something he is completely against, but it was nice to have a little panic that I'd be a mom and be able to teach them what I know. Adrien was in his early twenties when he got a vasectomy, knowing full well he didn't want children. He wasn't planning on getting married, either. He loved the single life of sleeping with whoever he wanted whenever he wanted. Then he met me that one rainy day and things changed. We're five years apart, but it doesn't feel like it. He doesn't treat me any less because I was barely an adult when we got together. He loves me. Not enough to reverse his vasectomy, but enough to love me unconditionally. Until eight days ago. Eight days ago he ended us without an explanation. One I don't think I want to know now.

"Wait one more week and see what happens," Silas suggests.

I lean into him and nudge his shoulder with mine. "At least we have some fun stuff to do in the meantime."

He rises, leaving a kiss on my head, and takes his coffee with him, leaving muffins on the table in its place. "I'll check the pharmacy for the morning-after pill." He sips his coffee. "They'll ask you a bunch of questions and request ID if you go in."

"Good idea."

He hesitates but kisses my lips quickly and makes his way to the pharmacy, saluting Anne on the way out. I watch him, what the fuck else am I going to do? He's so damn attractive, that it's hard to look away. He's a few inches taller than Adrien, but his robustness oozes confidence, even though he's so broken. Parts of me can't wait to ravish him and try to fix his sadness, other parts of me think I'm treading some dangerous territory. Christ, I need help.

My stupid and morbid curiosity takes over—I mean, why wouldn't it? As I said, I hate drama but I love the juice when it oozes. And it's really fucking oozing. I decide to reply to Adrien. Writing nothing more than, there isn't anything you can say that will make what you did any better.

As if he was waiting by his phone, he replies. Let me explain.

A growl rumbles through me, making me breathe heavily as I write back. You tried to have me killed you psychopath! Why the fuck would I want to talk to you?

Instantly, he replies again. Because it's me.

Tears well in my eyes. I love him. So fucking much. But he hurt me, badly. Betrayed me? Fucked me without plea-sure? Destroyed me? I don't even know what to say. I try to conjure up the courage to write back to him, but no words spill from my fingers. I stare at the blinking cursor as tears skim my cheeks. How could he do this to me? Everything we shared. All the laughs, the fights, traveling the world, sharing each other's secrets, diving into each other's minds, and the breathtaking sex...how could he even think about doing this to me? Was it that Parisian bitch who coaxed him into killing me with her croissant-making pussy?

WHAT THE FUCK DID I DO WRONG, ADRIEN?

After I silently break down, I compose myself, feeling that eerie sense that someone's watching me. Probably Anne. I look up, not Anne. She's not even paying attention to me. But that feeling doesn't leave. To my dismay, someone is looking at me. I glance up and see someone standing at the window. Their face is covered with a ski mask, and their black jacket and matching snow pants hide any ounce of flesh. The bright orange goggles stand out against the darkness of their outfit. They're just standing there, watching me.

I try to look away and focus on the screen before me, but their presence is so heavy, I can't help but glance at them again. The hair on the back of my neck rises as goosebumps and tingles flow through me. I'm scared. There's no fucking doubt about that.

Slowly, his hand raises, a black mitten covering it, and he waves. He knows I see him and he knows who the fuck I am. I jump from my seat, and back into the beam beside me, my heart leaping into my throat. I'm going to die for real very soon, and this is the fucking guy to do it. He moves slowly to the entrance of the café and I shoot my attention to Anne.

Where the fuck did Anne go? Fuck! Where is she?!

I quickly log out of my email and scope out the café for an exit strategy. No exits aside from the one this fucking creep is walking through. I slide down the beam and hold my head in my hands. I never followed or listened during Sunday School. It was forced upon me from the time I was able to learn. Yet here I am, reciting a Hail Mary in the hopes it'll save me.

"Excuse me," Silas says, making his way to me.

The man in the orange goggles and black snowsuit stops in his tracks, looking at me crying and shaking like a child having a nightmare, and disappears. Silas, you sexy son of a bitch. Thank you.

Silas' hand touches my shoulders, gripping them and I let out a sob and squeeze my head to my knees.

My breathing shudders. "Is he gone? Please tell me he's gone."

He pulls my hands away from my head, then touches my shoulders again. "Let's go home, okay?"

"Adrien." I start rocking back and forth. "I know that's one of his men. It has to be. I can't stay with you. I'm only putting you in danger."

"Parker, nowhere else is safe," he says, gripping my shoulders more firmly to stop my rocking. "Look at me, hmm?"

"No," I whisper, too afraid to look up.

He lifts my head. "There's no one here, Parker. Just Anne and a couple of customers."

I look up, he's right. There isn't a man in a black snowsuit and orange goggles. There's only a family sitting at a nearby table glancing over at us. It's official, I'm really losing it. "Didn't you see him?"

Silas tilts my chin up. "It was just the family, Parker."

I groan, sniffling. "Fuck."

He takes my hand, helping me rise to my feet. My legs feel like jelly. "C'mon."

Without another word, we leave. Driving quietly back to his house. Adrien, that asshole, he's toying with me. It's evident now. He tried to kill me and failed. Now all he has to do is torment me until I lose my mind and people start sympathizing with him thinking I cracked. I know what I saw. I saw that man staring at me. I'm not fucking crazy. I'm not.

*

The truck comes to a stop and Silas turns onto a different road than usual, looking in his rear-view mirror. He speeds up on the incline and glances at the rear-view mirror a few times, before turning onto another road and slamming on the gas.

I sit upright, alert. "What's going on? This isn't the way to your house."

He keeps his eyes between the road and his mirrors. "This car's been tailing us since we left Anne's."

I look behind us and who do I see other than that black car with stainless steel rims about six car lengths away. Silas slows down, the tail end of the truck skidding somewhat but regaining its grip and he takes another turn down a hill and then a sharp left onto a dirt road. He speeds up again, attempting to lose whoever is following us. It seems it's working. He takes another sharp right and revs up the incline to another left and drives into someone's driveway, parking in a brushy area and killing the engine. We both look back, wondering if we are still being followed. I knew I wasn't going crazy!

"I told you I shouldn't be with you," I whisper for some reason as if the car can hear me. "They know I'm with you and know your truck. This insanity."

"It'll be all right," he says, keeping his gaze out the back window and placing a reassuring hand on my thigh.

"They already hurt your dog—"

"If they knew where you were they'd have staked out my house, don't you think? Not stalk you in town," he interrupts me. "I told you, you're safe."

I wipe down my face, looking out the window and taking in the silence. But I'm not safe, they know I'm with Silas meaning they already know where he lives. "Shit."

What am I supposed to do? I'm a dead woman no matter what. But why? It can't be for my life insurance, can it? We have money. Adrien doesn't need money. What's your motive? Your reasoning here, Adrien?

He drops the keys in the cupholder and glances around once more. There isn't much to see other than bushes and sleeping trees. "I got an idea." He gets out of the truck.

I snag the sunglasses and follow him. "Silas?"

He makes his way up to the white house with blue shutters and taps on the red disheveled wooden door. I look behind me, I swear I can hear footsteps. They're running at me, their footprints pasted in the snow. But there's no one there. There never really is, is there? Frankly, the sounds of nature are all so new to me. I'm a city gal, and this silence is maddening.

An older man opens the door. "Yeah?" He has one shoe on, red flannel pants, and a thin undershirt with holes and stains on it. The stench of alcohol reeks off him and his five o'clock shadow has remnants of maple syrup on it. He's old, I'll give him that, the wrinkles on his face are so deep, dirt accumulates in them. He looks homeless as fuck.

"Murph, can I park my truck here? Was making a weird sound on the way back from Marty's. Gonna have Bob check it out when he's back next week," Silas says.

Murphy looks at me a moment as I nibble on my thumbnail. "Not a problem."

Silas grins at me. "Mind if we borrow Cathy's cruiser until then?"

Murphy kicks the door open. "Come in, I gotta find the keys for you."

"All right." Silas takes my hand and pulls me into the house with him.

It's cute on the outside and a fucking chaotic nightmare on the inside. There are stacks of used plates scattered around the area, beer bottles, and cans as well. It looks like the day after a frat party. The smell, though. Mothballs and sour milk with hints of either ketchup or barbecue sauce. I might hurl if I breathe this in any longer.

Clatter and bangs move through the house and Silas gives me a grin, putting his arm around my neck and pulling me in to kiss my head. I love it when Adrien does this move. It's so calming. My arms slide around Silas' waist and I let out a breath. I needed this to get me out of my head. Silas knows me so well and yet, barely knows me at all.

"Here we are," Murphy announces, coming back in with the keys. "Parking break doesn't work, but don't think you'll need it."

Silas lets go of me. "Thanks."

"Don't think we've met, I'm Murphy McFadden." He holds his hand out to me. Oh, God, I don't want to shake that crusted cesspool of germs. His fingers are yellow. Yellow! How is that even normal? I understand the roughness and the dirt from working, but yellow? Fuck, here comes the bile.

"Parker Smith," I reply, using my maiden name.

"About time he brings someone around." Murphy McFadden laughs. Such an Irish name for someone who has no accent or even light eyes. "You just move in?"

I adjust the sunglasses nervously. "Oh, um, no. I'm just visiting."

Murphy McFadden nudges Silas' shoulder. "Pretty little lady gonna get you outta the forest and into the big city again?"

"Time will tell." Silas puts his hand in mine. "Good to see you, Murph. I'll give Bob a call and have him pick up my truck. Keys'll stay in the cupholder if he asks."

Murphy nods. "No problem."

Silas leads us to a small light blue car I'm sure hasn't been used in years. He opens the door for me and the car reeks of stale cigarettes and sweat. So maybe it has been used, at least for sex. I clear my throat as Silas gets in the car and pulls out of the spot.

My heart's beating rapidly as we pull onto the road and I can't help but slouch in my seat as if hiding. They'll find me sooner or later. There's no use in hiding and I know I can't go into town anymore. Silas will have to go without me. Or I might have to leave him and find a place to hide out without risking his life.

I clench and unclench my fists. "My hands won't stop shaking."

"Are you sure you saw someone at Anne's?" he asks, and by the tone of his voice, he obviously doesn't believe me.

"I am."

He nods. "Mm."

I sniff, finally taking off the sunglasses. "I'm not crazy if that's what you're thinking."

He gives me a sly smile. "I wouldn't have slept with you if I thought you were."

"You slept with your ex-wife a bunch of times."

"I object," he says, laughing. I can't help but chuckle, too. He's pretty funny when he wants to be. At least when he puts down some walls and lets me in.

I lean my head back, still reeling from the day we've had. A cluster fuck of emotions has spread through me. It's ridiculous. "Did you get the pill?"

"None left. They have a few in the town over."

"Oh," I say, turning to him and chuckling. "Guess we can bareback it for another day and pick it up tomorrow."

"Yeah." He lets out another laugh, looking over at me with that look he's given me so many times since I've been here. As wrong as it should be to want to screw him right now, I can't help it. I cheated on my husband, but Adrien cheated on me, too, and I think his trying to kill me merits me some free passes.

Plus, this is how I deal with stress. I fuck. I cum. I release.

The tiny car pulls up to Silas' house, it is a cute house—aside from the abundance of fallen logs of wood and boarded-up windows. This must be heaven in the summer. Let's hope I don't stay here that long, I miss my memory foam mattress, my jacuzzi bath, my closet, and my kitchen.

My study used to be my sanctuary until Adrien took it over and started using it as his office. I'd curl up on the leather couch that cost way too much for how it feels to sit on—like cement—and study my scripts. As time went on, my bed became that place or the love seat by the fireplace in the guest room. I like being alone when I study the scripts. I feel like I have to channel the women I'm reading on the page and doing that alone is a must.

My mind is still spinning, I can't believe this shit is happening to me, of all people. I'm just an actress, nothing more than that. My parents aren't famous, my father's a preacher and my mother is insane. Adrien is the only person in my life to make me somebody. After all these years, it's clear I'm nothing but a play doll and a paycheck.

Silas lets me walk into the house first, and I'm barely able to take my boots off before he grabs me and kisses me. I'm taken aback at first. With everything that happened today, I doubted he'd want to have sex again. But here he is, his tongue sweeping my mouth and hands slithering my body.

I bite his lower lip and move away from him, letting his jacket fall from me. He grabs me again and spins me around, bending me over the dining room table. Fuck, yes, Silas! It's like he knows I love it rough.

I push off the table as his tongue touches my cheek. "That all you got?"

His hand grabs my crotch and scratches along the jeans until he grabs my ass. Jesus Christ, the way he's teasing me, I might explode before he even enters me.

As he nibbles my neck, his thumb snaps off the button of my jeans and he pushes them down, roughly grabbing my ass again before I hear his zipper. He doesn't even wait for me to be ready, he kicks my foot aside to spread my legs and roughly pushes inside me. He's savage, quick. God, he's so big right now it kind of hurts, but I don't fucking care. It feels too damn good to complain.

He shoves me down again, hurting me this time since my chin hits the table. I'll deal with the pain later.

No one has ever fucked me like this before. He thumps so rough, it's like he's releasing all the pent-up anger he's had inside him over the six years since his life crumbled. Take it out on me, Silas. Fuck me as hard as you want.

I gasp feeling him pull out of me, and he grabs a fist full of my hair. His tongue licks up my neck, sending a shiver through me before he spins me, pulling the sweater I'm wearing over my head and tearing off the t-shirt. Next to leave is my bra, but he doesn't undress. He stays in his puffy vest and checkered green shirt. I'm lifted onto the table and again, he shoves himself inside me, taking me as hard as he was before.

I don't even try to stay quiet, I let every pleasurable and painful moan out, and by the rose in his cheeks, I know he fucking loves this.

He grabs one of my breasts and suckles it, his cold hands make my nipples harder. I grip the back of his head and yank on his hair to move him away and kiss me. His kiss is even rough and savage. Goddamn. Without warning, he lets out a moan himself, slowing his pace down and breathing heavily. Even his moan is sexy.

He doesn't say anything when he finishes, just kisses me. His kiss isn't as rough anymore, it's soft and passionate. We're going to have some fun here.

I sigh and fall back on the table. "Jesus, fuck."

He leans his hands in fists to either side of me. "I was a little too rough, wasn't I?"

"I'll have you know, I like it rough." I let out a breath of air. "Just like that."

"Good." He takes off the puffy vest and checkered shirt, then smiles. "I have six years of build-up that need to come out."

I pull his face to mine. "Mm, then take it out on me, baby."

For a moment, I forget why I'm here. I forget the loss, the death, the fear. I forget because, for a moment, I'm in utter bliss.

CHAPTER 15

For almost an entire week, nothing happens around the house. We screw like teenagers on every piece of furniture he owns. Breaking two dining room chairs in the process. I feel alive for the first time in a long time, and Adrien and I used to screw like rabbits. There's just something about the way Silas looks at me, the way he talks, his demeanor, and ouff, the way he moans and grunts when we fuck, just thinking about it makes me wet.

He has me up against the bookshelf by the staircase. We're making out and I know in a minute we're going to lose our clothes and be one again. I can feel him push into me, moaning softly against my lips when a knock strikes the door. I keep his lips pressed on mine. There's no way in hell he's answering the door.

His grip on my bottom tightens, but by the second set of hard knocks, he groans and pulls away from me. Whoever is at that door better be dying. "One sec—"

"No, no, no, no, no," I whine.

He smiles, licking his lips. "Just stay here."

I keep my arms wrapped around his neck and chuckle softly. "No, baby, ignore them." My tongue drags up his jawline, nibbling his earlobe.

He groans, resting his forearm on the bookshelf behind us. "Mm, you're killing me." I kiss his neck again, biting as delicately as I can when knocks strike AGAIN. "Shit, one second."

Putting me down, he licks his lips and adjusts his white t-shirt. I stand by the bookshelf, out of the way but able to listen to what's happening and see as much as I can without being seen. A smirk is sent my way as he adjusts himself in his pants and opens the door to Billy—the local cop.

Billy nods, looking into the house before meeting Silas' gaze. He takes a paper from his pocket and unfolds it. "Morning, Silas."

"What can I do for you?"

"Parker Bailey," Billy replies, holding up a Missing Person's flyer I'm sure Adrien posted around town for some sympathy, the sick fuck. "We're asking everyone around the river again if they've seen her. Husband claims he saw her couple days ago."

"Husband sure?" Silas asks, folding his arms across his chest.

Billy looks into the house again. "He's still in shock from her death. Can't blame him for trying to make sure."

Is he for real? Still in shock? The last thing Adrien is in shock about is my death. He probably wants to find me and have his goons kill me, or plead with me not to rat him out to the press and ruin his precious company. Still in shock my fucking ass.

Silas shifts his weight from one foot to the other. "Papers say her body was found."

"Face was caved in. Could've been anyone that resembles her." Billy hands him the flyer. "But that's just my guessing. There's no way of telling without DNA testing."

And if they do DNA testing they'll find out the woman they found wasn't me.

"They doing that?"

Billy shrugs. "Not sure, body was picked up and transported to California for further investigating. Probably why the husband is still here trying to figure out what to do." He's pretty open with Silas about the case, I wonder if it's because he's a lawyer or if this is how Billy is with everyone.

Silas nods, scratching at his chin and revealing those hickies I left him last night. "Where's he staying?"

"Rental," Billy replies as if Silas knows exactly which house he's talking about.

Silas grunts and nods. Is Adrien staying in the house where it happened? How many rentals are on that side of the river? It suddenly dawns on me. Cheryl, my stunt double, was supposed to join me in Alaska after my birthday celebration. Could the woman they mangled be her? No. No, I won't believe it. I won't let myself believe that madness. But who the fuck did they kill?

"The girl you've been bringing into town, she know anything about this? Murphy said he met her, Anne, too. Said she got an earful from Louisa after meeting her. Mind if I meet her, too, and ask a few questions?" Billy looks over Silas' shoulder into the house. "They told me some things I just want to clarify."

Silas' jaw tightens. "What things?"

"Where is she?"

Silas tilts his head and narrows his eyes. "She's in the shower, you can come 'round later."

Is he for real? Billy gets one good look at me and he'll know I'm Parker fucking Bailey, the dead wife my so-called husband is looking for. I need to leave. It's official now. I need to speak with Jack and get the hell out of this frozen hell.

Billy takes the flyer from Silas and nods. "I gotta knock on a lotta doors today. I'll come by later in the week if she's still here." He leaves with a salute and he walks off, the snow crunching under his feet.

The door closes and I let out a disgruntled groan. I'm terrified of what will happen if the cops get ahold of me. Adrien is one powerful asshole, if he gets wind of where I am, I'll be permanently dead...instead of this weird limbo where the world thinks I'm dead and only a handful of people don't.

I wipe a hand down my face. "Well, fuck. Now what do I do?"

Silas peers out the window, watching Billy drive off. "I'll head into town, alone, and check your email. Maybe your brother wrote back."

"I should just go home. Show up and be like hey, I didn't die. My husband is a nut case who tried to kill me and...ugh, and I don't know. I just...I don't want you to get into trouble and the longer I stay here, I know you will. And who knows, maybe nothing will happen, but also, if it does, I don't want you hurt. Adrien's dirty side of the business is a mystery to me as it is to you, but I know he's fucking dangerous, and the men he hires are ex-cons who look for a way to legally do dirty without getting caught and put back in prison. Did you know he hires them as security? So when they show up to their parole officers or in court it just looks like they work for Bailey Incorporated and not the side of the business that involves threats, deaths, and so much blood and bullshit. I can't." I run my fingers through my hair and sit down at the table with my head in my hands. "Mm, nope. I can't deal with this shit."

"It'll be alright, I told you ain't nothing gonna happen to you," Silas says, placing his hands on my shoulders and kissing the top of my head.

"And I want to believe you—"

"Then do." He keeps his lips pressed to my head. "C'mere."

He pries my hands from my head and lifts me onto his lap, kissing my exposed shoulder a couple of times until I look at him. His jade-colored eyes are so piercingly bright in the shine from the snow through the window, it's like they can see right through me and all the thoughts running through my mind.

"I have to get out of this town, Silas. You know I'm right."

His head shakes slowly. "I know, I know...I just don't want you to leave."

"Then come with me? When's the last time you put your toes in the sand?"

He chuckles. "Let's get this settled before you whisk me away, darling."

"Mm, well, let's finish what we started before you head off to town, yeah?" I adjust myself on his lap so I'm straddling him.

"We already broke two of my chairs," he says between my kisses.

I pull the tank top over my head and shove his head into my cleavage. "Then let's make it three."

We screw all over the kitchen, finishing on the floor, breathless and sweaty. I'm not entirely sure what we are at all. But one thing I do know, is we know how to have sex. Oh, to be a fly on the wall in this house. It would be the perfect masturbation material for any horny fucker. My favorite is our shower sessions, he isn't scared to get dirty then. He'll cum on me or force me to my knees and have me suck him until he cums. Something about the showers makes him so much more experimental.

I'm so lucky and so disturbed at the same time.

I take a deep breath and look over at him as we're lying naked on our backs on the cool ceramic floors, and chuckle, letting my hand fall to his chest. He looks over at me, that smirk spreading to his lips, and takes my hand. "I'm really making up for lost time."

"How you went six years without having sex is beyond me," I say breathlessly. "Never had any flings with anyone in town?"

"Nope," he answers, still staring at me.

I bite my lower lip to stop myself from smiling too largely. "Is it 'cause I'm famous? That why you wanted to screw me?"

"You're gorgeous," he replies and leaves it at that. His eyes say so much more than his mouth ever could.

This is the difference between him and Adrien. Adrien spoils me with gifts and with words. He definitely does have a way with words, and the way he twirls his tongue a certain way—he'll tease me with it constantly just to get me to force him down so I can sit on his face and put that tongue to good use. His words were what got him to take control of the company and take the Bailey name into something so much bigger than it was. As much as I love Adrien, it feels like he's been all talk. Just to keep me around. To fuck me. To use me. To have me as arm candy at award shows and what have you.

Silas is a man of few words, but when he uses them, I listen and he never tells a lie. He always makes me feel beautiful. Adrien does, too, I can never take that away from him. Christ, he has a picture of me as his background on every device he owns and he stares at me in this way that drives me crazy. This is why I find it so hard to believe this whole situation. Why would he try to kill me if he loves me?

I finally look at Silas. "You're so different than I expected."

"What did you expect?" he asks, he still hasn't turned his attention away from me.

His eyes say so much more right now than they ever did. Tell me what's going on in that head Mister. Just a little. Let me in a little bit.

In time. He'll let me in when he's ready.

I want to tell him something that's circled my mind a couple of times. I don't know if he'll be offended by it, but I have to get it off my chest. "I thought you were in on it at some point during my stay."

He scoffs with a chuckle. "Well, thanks."

I laugh, blushing. "Sorry." I cover my face and shake my head. "I didn't know what to think when I woke up in your house."

Those eyes of his are smiling. Again, saying so much without opening his mouth. I don't think he cares that I suspected him. It only makes sense. Two weeks have gone by and I don't know who to point fingers at. There's my husband, but my brain is jumbled at the thought of him being responsible for my death. We shared too many moments for me to believe it. I'm confused and lost, and the only thing making me feel grounded, is this man beside me.

"Your husband's an idiot for ever letting you go."

My smile grows, bringing heat to my cheeks. "Why did we have to meet under these shitty-ass circumstances?"

He takes my hand and kisses my fingertips delicately. "Everything happens for a reason."

I glance at the ceiling, scared to ask him this. I believed Adrien and I were endgame. There was never anything other than us. Now, all I see is a future with this mountain man. "After all this is over, where does that leave us?" I slowly turn my head to see his answer through those eyes.

"Wherever you want."

Wherever I want, huh? Not the answer I was looking for since I want a lot of things right now. But being with him is truly all I can ever hope for. I like this and I'm happy I like this, I just hope he likes this, too.

I turn onto my stomach and rest my head in my hand. "So you're really leaving me all alone in this house in the middle of the woods?" I have to change the subject, I don't want to dive into what we can be when I'm still confused as fuck.

Silas is heading into town to see if my brother wrote back. I hope he did. I need something positive to come out of this fear.

He chuckles, "I'll be gone no more than thirty minutes. You can stay naked and wait for me to get back. He turns into me and slaps my ass before he lies on top of me.

I bite my lip as he bites my shoulder. "I like that idea."

"Good," he says kissing my shoulder blades and sliding a hand to my stomach to lift me.

I feel him growing on my leg. How does he have so much energy? He remains lying on top of me, parting my legs and sliding inside me. He doesn't last long, not enough for me to even get into it, but it still feels good. And I adore the way he grabs my ass every time he's about to cum. Jeez, I get tingly and aroused just envisioning it. He lifts us onto our knees and separates my cheeks to get a good look at what he's doing. I drip some more to be able to see what he sees. Yes, I get it, I'm one horny fuck.

After we finish, we dress slowly, his eyes eating me up and suckling each breast before I tuck them away. Adrien opened up my sexually deviant side. I was stale before I met him, sex missionary or me on top. Now I'm a sex addict, thanks. He changed me in so many ways. Looking back, I wonder if he controlled me just because I was desperate for fame.

Silas takes my hand and leads me to the bookshelf. Removing a couple of books and taking out a gun. Why is he taking out a gun? Is this for me? The fuck am I going to do with a gun? Yeah, I've used prop guns before on set, but I've never used a real one.

"Silas?" I say, nerves evident in my tone.

He holds it out to me. "You know howta use it?"

My breathing tremors. "Why would I need to use it?"

"I'm leaving you alone for a little, just in case you feel scared, this here will protect you." He spins the barrel and pops it back in place. "Right here, that's the safety. It's on now, but with a simple click, see, it's off and you can use it. This right here is to cock the gun. Simple and easy. Point, aim, shoot. Got it?"

"Point. Aim. Shoot," I repeat, then shake my head. "I don't want a gun."

"Okay." He steps over to the table and leaves it there. "It's right here."

I bite my lower lip anxiously. "Please don't take too long."

"I won't," he says, taking the piece of paper from the table with my email and password on it. "Want anything from Anne's?"

"No, just hurry up."

He bops under my chin. "What you can do is start cutting up the veggies and meat for the stew I'm making tonight."

"And just like that, I'm a housewife."

He does nothing but laugh and pulls me in for a kiss, not even a goodbye as he walks to the car and speeds off. I'm alone. In this quiet-ass house, I'm alone.

Sound stands still here. There isn't a honking horn, no laughter or conversations in the distance, no seagulls squawking, just dead silence. The wind howls, and it's like I can hear Mother Nature blowing it from her lips. The way the gust moves the naked branches of the trees is even eerie. Sounds like someone wrestling to get loose from the branches. Oh, please hurry the fuck up, Silas.

I let out a breath and look around, the soft crackling of fire reminds me to add more firewood to it or else we'll freeze tonight. I toss in a couple of logs, watching as sparks and embers move around and slowly catch the new logs. The flames grow and a smile touches my face. I miss this type of serenity. No phone. No internet. No social media. No premiers or red carpets. No interviews. No photoshoots. It's just me being me. I love it so much. I feel free.

The boxes that Louisa brought for Silas are still sitting by the staircase. I'm curious to know what's inside. I also want to respect his privacy, but hey, he's been inside me how many times? We've slept in the same bed for how many nights?

I step closer to the boxes and peer inside. There are some of his lawyer books, photos of his family, a couple of photos of him and his son, a few of his shirts and jewelry, and endless knickknacks. Nothing special. He's a simple man, yet Louisa's words still circle my mind.

Then I remember the envelope under the bed. My curiosity spikes and I go for it, knowing it's none of my business, but I also want to know why it's under the bed. I go to climb the stairs and the creak echoes, making me jump. Fuck, it's quiet here. I'm scaring myself with every creaking footstep I take.

Silas fixed the bed yesterday, but I still haven't slept in it. We've been sharing his bed, sleeping naked so we could slip in a quickie in the middle of the night, or have our morning glories as soon as we rise. Mmph, he doesn't know how much the sex excites me. I'm a pervert when it comes down to it, and I'm not even shy to admit it. Adrien knows how dirty my mind is, and it's only a matter of time before Silas gets used to it. Sex is my release. Not therapy, not yoga, or massages. Just wild sex.

I get on my knees beside the bed and look under it. It's not there. Louisa didn't take it because I saw it after she left. Silas, what are you hiding?

I growl and start searching the room. I open empty drawers, I rummage through the closet, and I even start tapping on the floorboards in case there's a hollow one to hide things. Nothing.

I check his room. I don't care if it's an invasion of privacy. I have to know what that envelope is. His room is full of crap. So many knickknacks and bar paraphernalia. It's probably from his bachelor pad before he got hitched to a woman he didn't love only because she was pregnant.

I open drawers, look behind picture frames, and inside some of the bar mugs. Christ, I even check between the mattress and the box spring. Nothing. All I find are endless buttons, socks folded so nicely, his clothes folded at the most precise ninety-degree angle, lawyer books, two guns I have no business finding, and our condom stash.

There's nothing here. Goddamnit. Could Louisa be right? Am I missing something and am clouded by his sexual deviance to see between the lines?

I give up. There's no use in snooping anymore. But I will ask him about it. If he says nothing was there, then I know he's lying...but what am I trying to prove? I don't even know what the envelope is. Maybe it was the divorce papers. Or the certificate of death for his son. Fuck. Why am I so sick and twisted that I have to know these things?

I go back downstairs and decide to finish the book I started when I got here. I never read, but this one particular story has me hooked. A high school girl with telekinetic powers? Count me in!

Before I even make it off the last step, I hear footsteps from the hallway where Silas and I shared our first kiss. I look and see those orange goggles again right outside the backdoor.

Jesus, fuck. Silas, where are you!?

The back door opens like nothing. Does he have a key? Expert lockpicker? Shit! I charge up the stairs and stop. I swear I can't breathe. Everything around me shoots into focus. I hear the sweat form and trickle on my temples, the hair rising on the back of my neck, and my heart rapidly beating.

They're in the house. I hear their footsteps moving along the floorboards. Like an idiot, I left the gun downstairs.

I move as stealthily and quietly as I can, sneaking into Jack's bedroom and getting into the crawl space in the closet.

Heavy footfalls travel through the house. From the living room to the open kitchen and the bathroom...they stop at the bottom of the steps and open the front door. Another set of footsteps comes in and starts for the stairs.

Fuck! Fuck! Fuck!

The guest room, the hallway closet—shit! The door to Jack's room opens and the footsteps stop, standing in the doorway.

I can't see a thing in this crawl space, but goddamn, being in the darkness—it's like anything could be in here with me.

Breath caresses my face, but no one is there.

Hands grab me, grip my mouth, and squeeze my neck, but no one is there.

I'm falling but I can't move from my spot.

I'm hidden but I feel like I'm standing right out in the open for them to find me.

I blink a couple of times, trying to see in the darkness but I can't see a damn thing.

A chuckle leaves the person standing in the doorway, and I know that chuckle all too well. Adrien, you son of a bitch.

I try not to move as another set of heavy footfalls come toward the closet. I hold my breath, hearing the door to the closet open and the clothes move around. Goddamn it, please don't see this little door. Please. Please. Please.

"Parker!" Adrien yells. I squeeze my eyes shut as if doing so will stop him from seeing me.

"She's not here. I told you I saw them leave," orange goggles says.

"Argh!" Adrien punches the doorframe, letting out a grunt. The footsteps retreat to the master bedroom and washroom, then head back downstairs.

"I'll check the grounds," orange goggles says.

"No. Let's head back to town," Adrien says, then silence takes over the bottom floor.

I don't move until I hear the front door open and shut. A car starts and drives off in the distance. They are gone and yet I can't move. My body is shaking and I'm hyperventilating, yet I can't fucking move.

Fifteen minutes go by of me weeping as quietly as I can until I finally build up the courage to get out of the crawl space. The home is just as eerily quiet as it was before. All I have to do is quietly make my way to the kitchen, grab the gun, and wait for Silas, he'll be here very soon. I hope he'll be here very soon.

There doesn't seem to be anyone in the house as I creep down the stairs, the gun is in sight and it'll be perfect. I'll lunge for it and keep it ready for—I don't know. But I'll keep it ready.

I look down the hallway to the back door. It's clear, empty. Phew. I grab the gun from the table and I feel it. That stare, that longing. I don't even have time to look up.

Adrien grabs onto my arms to try and tries to pry the gun from me.

I yelp, struggling against his strength. Then it dawns on me. He dislocated his knee six years ago. It flares up in bad weather or on planes from the pressure; one hit and he'll be down for the count.

I don't even think, I back-kick his knee and he belts in agony, letting go of me and the gun, and falling to the floor. I hold up the gun and back into the kitchen. Cock, point, aim.

I can't shoot. I can't.

"What the fuck, Adrien?"

"Why the fuck would you hit my knee?!" he screams. He's holding onto it and tears, actual tears are falling from his eyes.

I sniffle, letting the tear fall and drip off my chin. "You tried to kill me."

"I can explain, babe, I swear. Please, baby, please. Just let me explain," he says through deep breaths. I keep the gun on him and grab a bag of frozen corn from the freezer.

Helping him into one of the chairs, I guide his leg onto another and place the frozen corn on his knee. I back away, keeping the gun firmly in hand, and sniffle again, staring at him as if I have no idea who he is. "I thought you loved me. We were endgame, weren't we?"

"We are. I promise we are, babe, just listen, okay?" he groans, trying to move his leg, but leaves it and meets my eyes. "I had no choice."

"Seriously? No choice? That's what you're fucking excuse is?" I raise my voice. Is this guy for real? I start crying, unable to hide the fact that I'm hurt and shake my head. "Everyone has a choice. I'm your wife! You could've chosen not to kill me."

"My dad." He cries with me. "He made me—"

"Who did you kill?"

"I didn't kill anyone," he whispers, dragging in a breath to explain his stupid self. "They drugged me and the next thing I remember it's New Year's morning and I'm half-naked lying in an empty bed in Alaska. I looked around for you, thinking I got way too drunk and you just decided to bring us to Alaska earlier. You know how I hate to fly." He sniffs, looking me up and down. "But you weren't there. Then I saw blood and broken glass and called the cops. They arrived right as I was giving you mouth-to-mouth. Your face was caved in, you were a block of ice, but I had to try. I had to save you—but as soon as they pulled me off you, I realized it wasn't you." He shakes his head, holding onto his knee. "It was Cheryl," he whispers, then sniffs again and looks up at me. "And after hours of interrogation, my father's men show up and explained the situation."

I scoff, the gun shaking in my grip. "What situation?"

"Explained what happened," he corrects himself, eyeing the gun.

"That you tried to kill me?" I shout.

He weeps, looking so small right now. Not the confident Adrien I know. Not the man everyone turns their heads to when he walks into a room. He's not commanding this room. I am. "I didn't."

"I don't believe you. You told me if I ever show my face again it'll be the last thing I do!"

He wipes his eyes and groans, trying to move his leg. "They tapped my phone."

"Who was that woman?"

He gulps, meeting my eyes with that guilt washing over him. "What woman?"

I grit my feet and step forward. "Don't play dumb with me."

He puts his head down and sobs. He's the most vulnerable I've ever seen him. "Cloé."

"How long has that been going on?"

His shoulders hunch; disappointment and betrayal oozing out of him as disgust washes over me. "She came to see me a few days after news broke to the public that you were dead."

"How long?" I grit my teeth, raising the gun higher. "Fucking look at me!"

He lifts his head immediately, those big eyes filled with shame and tears. "We kissed when you were at the premiere in France last year. It meant nothing—" He sobs when he sees the anger bloom in my cheeks, holding the frozen corn on his knee. "She stayed in touch and when news broke..." I choke a sob, but it's not working. I'm crying and I'm just as guilty as he is. "We had sex—a tension reliever—but I told her to leave me—"

My heart is squeezed, then tossed on the ground and stomped on. "I can't believe you."

He bangs his fist on the table. "I thought you were dead!"

"So the first thing you do is fuck someone else?"

He shakes his head quickly, holding his hand out to me, but I don't take it. I don't want to take it even though my head is telling me to hold his hand. He'll make the pain go away. "They told me they took care of you so I would get your life insurance—"

I fucking knew it.

I slap his hand out of the way, tears streaming down my face. "So the second you think I'm dead you move on?" I scream.

"No, baby," he cries.

I roughly wipe my cheek. "I thought you loved me."

"I do love you. I will always love you," he yells. "You're my muse, my woman, my everything."

"You let them try and kill me..." I lower the gun, my arm is weak and heavy. But when I look at his lips, I imagine them on that woman in France last year. While I was faking a smile at a premier I didn't even want to go to, he was kissing another woman. I raise the gun and snarl. "...for fucking money!"

"I had no choice. I didn't know what was going on until after I found Cheryl. I spent hours trying to tell them what happened to me. No one believed me until my father's men came and tried to take me home. I couldn't leave. I had to find you, especially after that phone call you made. I had to pretend to threaten you and tell them it was some crazed fan prank calling again." He sniffs, shaking his head. "Colm was in debt. All this was to pay off my father's debts."

I'm fuming, finger hesitating on the trigger as I stare at this man who has lied to my face for years. "All this because of debts?"

"I'm sorry."

I am so livid, so disturbed, so unforgiving. I want him to know how mad I am, to know his stupidity will never go unnoticed. He stares at me, tears still skimming his cheeks, and I can tell he wants to come to me and hold me. Kiss me like he's going off to war. I don't move, I stare at him and tell him the one thing I know will hurt him. "I fucked the guy who saved my life."

Anger blooms in an instant. "Why the fuck did you do that for?"

I raise the gun higher. "Why the fuck would you screw that French bitch?"

He breaks down, covering his face and sobbing. "I thought I lost you."

"So you fuck her?" I shout.

He lifts his head, snot mixed with tears covering his face. "You fucked him!" he shouts back.

I growl, baring my teeth. "And I fucking loved it."

His face softens and he wipes his nose on his sleeve, sniffling and looking off at the crackling fire in the living room. "Why would you do this?"

Okay, wait. Is he seriously mad at me? His father tried to kill me. He fucked that French bitch who he kissed while we were still together. Get your priorities straight, Adrien.

"I...you tried to have me killed," I say softly.

"I didn't. Baby, look at me. You know me better than anyone." Those amber-colored eyes of his are so deceiving yet I find myself believing him.

I know his father. Colm's a manipulative and controlling asshole.

"Fuck," I let out, starting to cry again.

"Parks, come here."

I don't move. My body takes a step forward, but I stop my heart from winning. "What happened to us? You've been so distant with me lately. Did you know this was going to happen to me?" There's so much desperation in my tone, I'm afraid if he tells me he loves me again, then I'll believe every single thing he says.

"I thought if I tried to hate you and distance myself from you, then it would be easier. I kissed Cloé thinking it would help. It didn't. It wasn't easier. I love you, Parker. I'll always love you. I shouldn't have agreed to this. But I was scared of what they'd do to you if I wasn't involved." He stares at me, taking in my reaction.

He does it. He says he loves me. But I'm too in shock to register.

He knew they would kill me and he let it fucking happen? How in the hell am I supposed to mentally recover from this blow?

He sniffs, wiping his eyes. "You weren't supposed to be hurt, baby. I was going to tell you on New Year's Day over breakfast. The plan was to fake your death so that I'd get your life insurance." He shakes his head. "They wouldn't let me tell you. Colm wouldn't let me tell you." He gulps. "It was supposed to happen on your birthday." He grits his teeth. "But they fucking drugged us and changed shit around because they knew I wouldn't go through with it."

I push my lips together and hold in a whimper, he doesn't deserve to see how hurt I am. But I'm fucking gutted. Inside I'm screaming, I'm hitting him, I'm letting my fingers pull the trigger. But on the outside, I'm not doing anything. I'm just staring at him, taking in all the information.

I wipe my eyes, holding my composure the best I can. Why can't I explode? Why won't I let myself explode? "How did you know where I was?"

"People in town said the guy living here was with some chick and he never brings anyone around. I had a feeling it was you," he says, furrowing his eyebrows. "I mean, who wouldn't recognize you, baby? You're the most beautiful woman in the world—"

I let out a breath. "Save it."

Our eyes lock and neither of us says anything. We just cry. We cry because even though it hasn't been said out loud yet.

It's over. Our love-filled days are over because of his father. If Adrien trusted me enough to let me in on the bad side of the business, maybe we wouldn't be in this situation. But we are. We're living it and we're going to be living our lives without each other in it from now on.

I glance out the window, spotting Silas pulling in. "You hurt his dog, y'know. You didn't have to do that."

"That was my dad's guys. Babe, you know me."

I glance out the window again and see Silas get out of the car, frowning as he sees me, gun in hand with tears sliding down my cheeks. He bursts into the house, causing Adrien to flinch and put his hands up.

Silas comes for me and grabs the gun, pointing it at Adrien. His hands are up and he's looking at me, pleading without saying a word.

Silas looks back at me, putting his free arm in front of me as protection. "What the fuck's going on?" My hand touches his protective arm and his tense shoulders relax.

"I'm here to see my wife," Adrien barks.

"You tried to have her killed!" Silas barks back.

Adrien begins to cry. "I didn't." His shoulders hunch and he sobs into his hands. I hate seeing him this broken. I want to go to him, hold him, and fix things. But that wouldn't be right. It's not my place anymore.

I squeeze Silas' arm. "It wasn't him." Am I seriously believing this asshole right now? "He's telling the truth." Yep, I'm believing my asshole husband right now.

Silas gawks back at me, astounded by what I'm saying. "What?"

I seriously can't believe myself right now. "His father's a crook, a gambling addict, and an overall fuckhead. He apparently tricked Adrien. Had someone try to kill me just to collect the money and pay off the debts the company is in...it sounds insane...I don't think...I don't know what to think." I look at Adrien and his lower lip tremors. "He wouldn't hurt me."

Silas scoffs. "You're joking, right?"

I shake my head and wipe my cheeks. "I wish I was."

Silas raises his voice. "You can't believe this nut job!"

Adrien lets out a cackle. "Nut job? Says the guy who accepted five hundred thousand dollars to keep his mouth shut."

I gasp. "What?"

"I didn't know it was for this!" Silas screams.

I pull his arm to me. "Silas?"

What the actual fuck is happening right now?

Adrien adjusts the frozen corn on his knees and groans, scowling at Silas. "My father borrowed money and gave Silas half a million to keep his mouth shut if he saw anything because of how close he is to the rental we're staying at. There're two other houses Dad paid off on this side of the river."

"I don't understand."

"What's not to understand? He was paid to stay quiet and then when he saw something, he took you in and tried to keep you here, didn't you?" Adrien thunders.

"I've been trying to help her." Silas takes the safety off the gun. "I saved her damn life."

Oh, shit. Oh, shit. Oh, shit.

He's going to kill my husband. Silas is going to fucking shoot Adrien.

"Why won't you let her use your phone?"

Silas's arm is so steady holding that gun it's terrifying. "I ain't got one. I told her that. That's why we go into town to use the computers and the phone there." He nods slowly. "But you knew that already. You followed us around town."

I'm covering my mouth trying to take in the severity of the situation. The madness. "Wait...you said your dad was bankrupt? How did he have money to pay Silas?"

"I told you." Adrien wipes his nose. "He borrowed it."

"You're lying," I say quietly.

"I'm not." Adrien whimpers. "Parks, I'm not. He called the Belizzos."

I let go of Silas' arm and meet his side glance. "Why would you accept the money?"

"I thought it was for a movie. Guy handed me a duffle bag filled with envelopes of money and a business card that said Bailey Industries on it. I'd have to be an idiot not to know who they are. You even told me you were filming a movie here, didn't you?" Silas answers angrily. "I thought they were paying me off to use my property for some shots."

"You could've told me," I say softly.

He shrugs a shoulder, apologies written all over his face. Why the fuck did he hide that important piece of information from me?

Adrien nods, looking between Silas and me. "I wouldn't lie to you, babe, you know that."

"I can't handle this," I say, putting a hand on my head and charging out the door. I need air, a second to breathe. What the fuck's happening right now?

I storm out without a jacket, bile rising in my throat as I stomp in the snow. Goosebumps completely cover my arms, engulfing me. I don't even know what to do, I just know I need out. So I walk, then I walk some more. I end up by the water where Silas found me. It's peaceful here. Too peaceful.

Adrien knew about it, Silas knew something was up, Colm wanted me dead...how can I even begin to process this soap-opera life I'm living.

I'm suffocating.

I'm drowning.

I.

Can't.

Breathe.

Footfalls echo behind me, charging at me and I tense up, preparing to be shot, pushed into the water, and drowned—for real this time. This is all too much and all too chaotic. I don't know what to believe.

Arms wrap around me and I inhale. He came for me when he didn't have to.

Silas is taking his flannel shirt off and draping it around me, no mind if he's shirtless on this freezing afternoon. I'm tense, I'm distraught. What is there to believe?

"You don't actually believe him?" he whispers, kissing my head.

I place my hand on his chest, whimpering softly. "Part of me does. I know him better than anyone. He wouldn't lie to me."

He grits his teeth. "This is fucked."

"Why wouldn't you tell me about the money?"

He wipes a tear from my cheek, leaving a soft hiss in its place. "I didn't know it was for this."

"You're not lying to me?" I ask, boring into his eyes.

"No," he whispers.

"Promise me."

He rests his head on mine. "I promise."

"What do I do?"

He lets out a breath, the air clouding around us. I've been dying to go home, dying to get out of this cold and into the sun that kisses my face every morning as I have my coffee and watch the waves crash onto the shore. Nothing is keeping me here, nothing but the jade-colored eyes boring into mine.

"You run," he says, holding my face in his hands.

I scoff. "Where the fuck am I supposed to go?"

"Your brother wrote back. He flew out and said to call him." He lets go of me and reaches into his back pocket for his wallet. He takes out a wad of cash, tucks it into my jeans, and puts a piece of paper into my other pocket. "Here."

This is it, isn't it? My life will forever be changed and this nightmare that turned into something so much more will be over. I sniff. "Silas?"

"Drive straight outta town and take exit seventeen south, the place he's staying is a few miles from there. Right by the McDonald's...you can finally fix this mess—"

"Come with me?"

"I have to make sure they don't follow you," he replies, wiping tears from under my eyes.

"But—"

He grunts, interrupting me. "Go down this path until you hit the water and cross to the other side. Murph's place is right there. Take my truck, all right?"

"Silas."

"Just go," he says, kissing me one last time.

I start to cry against his lips. "I can't."

"Go, darling." He leans his forehead on mine. "I'll be right here waiting."

Shots fire from behind us and he whips around, grabbing me and kissing me once more before he takes the gun from his back pocket.

"Wait!"

"Go, Parker!" he barks, the worry on his face is frightening me.

So I go, I trek along the path until I find that big red truck. I run until the pain of leaving someone who's changed me, weakens and I'm able to move on.

CHAPTER 16

I approach the motel, still reeling over what happened to me. I can't even begin to describe it. And every time I try to make sense of things, I start to cry. What am I supposed to do?

I clear my throat and approach the man my little brother has become. "Jacks?" He stands outside the motel room with Brody smoking a cigarette.

Jack gasps, his face drained of its color. He hesitates, taking me in for the first time in ten years, then charges for me. "Parks? Jesus, Parks. You're here. You're right here."

He holds me so tightly that I can feel the eleven-year-old boy in him come out with his sobs. He's sobbing into my neck and towering over me by at least eight inches. My little brother is all grown up and I have no words to describe what I'm even feeling right now.

Elated? Relieved? Sad?

No, right now, I'm so damn broken that this reunion with my brother is barely affecting me.

"Get me home," I say, nuzzling my face into his neck. "Please, Jacks."

Brody steps forward, nodding slowly, and flicks his cigarette. "It won't be easy. I need some time."

Seeing me is proof enough that this whole situation got a whole lot more interesting.

We make our way into their motel room and I spill my story. I tell them everything. I explain what happened with Silas, and what Adrien told me. I tell them about Colm, about Marlow, about Jackie and Louisa. Every little thing spills from my lips.

Jack holds me as I cry, kissing my head and rubbing my arm. "It's okay, Parks."

"I'm sorry," I sob.

He chokes on a sob. "I forgive you."

"I love you, kid."

"Let's get you home," he says, kissing my head.

Brody sputters, nodding and reading over the notes he took. Getting me home will be a challenge, but it's a possibility. Getting my life back to normal is a possibility. I can't say that doesn't make me happy.

"How's Mom? Dad?" I ask as Brody takes a blanket from the bed and wraps it around me.

I'm still shaking from the events of this morning, and shivering from the cold.

"They'll be happy to see you," Jack says, holding me tightly.

I sniffle, chuckling softly. "You have a beard."

He laughs, it is deep and booming. "I'm a pretty hairy fucker, you'd be surprised how many ladies like that."

I cover my face. "No, don't say that. The last time I saw you, you were wearing Spongebob pjs."

He kisses my head again. "Things are different, Parks. But things will change. You're coming home and I don't give a shit if you don't want to. You'll come to every birthday and holiday, ad stupid church event that Mom throws. You're home, Parks." He sniffs, choking a sob. "You're home."

I thought my ending was tragic. That I lost everything I earned. Everything I did. I didn't. My ending isn't tragic. It's changed. It's filled with love. Filled with possibilities. My ending is truly the beginning.

EPILOGUE

T hree Months Later

I was able to fly out a couple of days later, and finally go home. Adrien was arrested as were a slew of his security guards and Colm, of course. I haven't seen or spoken to Silas in three months. All I wonder is if he's okay. There's no way for him to contact me, and I have no idea what his address is or how to get to his house. Maybe it's for the better. He can go on with his life and his dog, and I can reimagine mine outside of the spotlight.

The verdict is in. Adrien made a plea deal and plead guilty. No trial. He is charged with knowledge of the attempted murder, or something like that, and is only sentenced to two years in prison. The fuckheads who killed my stunt double are there for life. Colm, well, he's on the run. No one has seen him or heard from him since New Year's Eve. Just my luck isn't it?

I didn't know what to believe, so I told the lawyers that Adrien was innocent in all of this—probably why he only got two years. I'm sure if I visit him, he'll be begging for my forgiveness once again. Maybe things will be different outside the fame. Maybe I can be a mom or a world traveler living out of my backpack. Whatever my decision, I'm definitely going to take a break from this whole actress thing. Alaska opened my eyes to living life again. It was the break I knew needed to happen.

Pressure is lifted from me, and I don't know what to do with myself.

My agent has asked me to do a couple of interviews, so I agree that I'll do one. Only one and tell everyone my plan to take a break. I don't want to see anyone now, nor do I feel like talking about this madness. But that's what being famous entails. Someone has to clear up the reality of the situation and tell the world the truth. My truth.

Claps and cheers echo behind the curtain. I always hated doing interviews. There would be allotted questions we went over and I approved of, but the interviewers never abided by them. Being put on the spot isn't my forte. I tend to let my emotions speak for themselves. I'm scared it will happen today.

"Our next guest has been through hell and back—or should I say, rose from the dead," Ms. Serena says, pausing for dramatic effect. "Please welcome, Parker Bailey."

I let out a breath and put my face on—I'm an actress right, I do what I do best and smile even though I'm aching on the inside.

The crowd goes wild as I step onto the stage, waving at the roaring fans, and hugging Ms. Serena before sitting down.

I've done countless interviews for her before. What celeb hasn't? She's the go-to woman people open up to and tell their darkest secrets—a little fun and games added to the mix as well.

I cross one leg over the other. "Hi."

"Wow, you have been through one helluva roller coaster ride." Ms. Serena looks out at the crowd, then back at me for my answer.

I laugh. "You're telling me." Ugh, I hate my fake laugh. I sound like a hyena. Well, maybe not that chaotic, but anyone who knows me knows this isn't my laugh.

"How have you been dealing with everything going on? It must've taken a toll on you emotionally, spiritually, and physically."

The audience falls silent. Great. All eyes and ears are on me and I don't know what to fucking say.

How do I put any of this into words? "It's been an interesting few months."

"With Colm Bailey still at large, are you worried at all?"

I shake my head. "No." And it's true. I'm not worried one bit. If he comes back into the spotlight, he loses all the money that he cashed out and he gets to spend the rest of his life rotting in prison. Colm is not going anywhere and he will not pop out of the shadows to finish the job. I know my father-in-law well enough for that. He's planted his ass on some deserted beach somewhere south.

"If Adrien were here right now, what would you say to him?" Ms. Serena asks.

I scratch the back of my neck. "I don't know what I would say. He was put in a predicament he shouldn't have been put into. His father is one powerful man and owed certain people a lot of money. He declared bankruptcy without telling Adrien. And Adrien stupidly told his father about my life insurance policy...I still love my husband. A part of me always will, but he played no part in what happened to me. The only thing he's guilty of is a big mouth...I've moved on and am healing from my experience. And have to thank each and every one of my friends, my family, and all my adoring fans. I wouldn't be able to get through any of this without your kind words and continued support."

Ms. Serena claps and pouts her lips with a nod as she stares out at the audience. "When Adrien gets out of prison, will you two get back together?"

I take a breath. "As much as I love him and want to go back to the way things were, it's a conversation we do have to have. He may not have been involved, but his father did this to me. He tried to have me killed and had one of my closest coworkers killed instead. I can't just live with that."

Adrien and I did speak. We sat down and had a long conversation before they took him to prison. We spoke about the future and what that would hold for us when in reality, the only thing we needed at that moment was a good fucking to release our aggression. We did nothing of the sort and spoke, laying the cards on the table. He told me when he gets out, he's reversing the vasectomy and we'll have babies. As many as I wanted. He'll give up the company, sell its shares, sell our multiple homes, and move to this little house we once rented in Scotland. It was so beautiful and so tranquil. It took us an extra week to convince ourselves to leave. He said we'd be us forever and always without the spotlight. I love this thought, but I couldn't agree with it. I couldn't say yes because all I remember is waking up in a house that wasn't mine to a man I didn't know, only to read the headlines of a tabloid and discover I was killed. Adrien said everything I wanted him to, yet I couldn't agree to it. Not then anyway.

I wet my lips. "But I am taking a much-needed break from acting. I haven't decided how long, though. I need this to reconnect with my family and spend time with my friends. I need this for many other reasons, too. It'll be nice to breathe for the first time in eight years."

Ms. Serena pauses for dramatic effect and looks at her cards. "You have been nonstop since you and Adrien wed."

I nod. "I have, and with everything that's been going on...it's time."

"There was someone who helped you in Alaska, wasn't there?" she asks, folding her arm up on the armrest and tapping her finger to her lips a couple of times. This is her tactic. She does this when she thinks she's about to strike a nerve.

There wasn't much of my story that I hid from the world. I told everyone about Silas, keeping his name and history to myself, however. I told them about most of our experience, our connection.

I look down at my folded legs and a smile touches my lips. "Mm, there was."

"Do I detect a little secret romance?"

It's obvious from my blushing face something happened. "That's a part of my experience I don't want to express in full detail."

She inches forward. "No, do tell."

"I think my personal life has been in the spotlight for long enough, it doesn't need any more attention," I say, chuckling. When all I want to do is tell the world about Silas.

*

The interview went well. People were laughing, awing, and oohing where appropriate. I forced my laughs, I forced my smiles because all I wanted to do was cry. I still cry myself to sleep at night just replaying the whole situation.

And Silas. I think about him every day. I put his name on the list at the gate just in case he ever wanted to visit. If he ever did. I sometimes wonder if I should fly out to see him, see how things are or how he is. I'll never go because I don't think he'll want to see me. I don't know why, but this is how I think.

After the interview, I head home. I need silence and peace.

I pull into my house and can't wait to kick off these heels and sit on my porch to watch the waves crash. The home feels empty, though. I've been alone in this house before, but something doesn't feel right. Adrien isn't here and he won't be here for a while. I can't even call him and speak to him. My friends have moved on with their lives. My brother has gone home after staying with me for over a month and a half. Alexis is in Europe for Fashion Week, much to her dismay. She wanted to stay, but I insisted. We all need to move on at some point.

I go to the back of the house and unlock the two glass doors to let in the ocean breeze when my breath is caught in my throat. Silas is sitting on my porch, a duffel bag at his feet. His hair is coiffed and spiked at the front and his beard is shaved, only a five o'clock shadow remains.

He jumps to his feet the moment the doors open and gives me a once-over. He's never seen me this dolled up in person before. "Hi," he says.

Neither of us can move.

"What're you doing here?" I ask breathlessly. "How did you find me?"

"Your house is on the Map of The Stars tourist attraction." He places the pamphlet down on the lounge chair he was sitting on. "Lucky for me, you put my name on the list at the gate. Security let me right on in."

"Oh," I say, licking my taupe-painted lips.

"You look good."

I shimmy my shoulders a little. "Clean up well, don't I?"

He grunts, giving me another glance before he looks off to the horizon. "This whole area, it's yours?"

"Yeah, it's supposed to be private, but paparazzi sometimes trespass."

Silence spreads between us. We're speechless. Shocked. Yet he's not looking at me. He's staring at the ocean. I've told him about how peaceful it is to stare at it, how I get lost in the sound of the waves.

I've dreamt of this moment for months. Wondered what our reunion would be like. But it wasn't like this in my dreams. No, in my dreams I'd run to him and wrap my arms around his neck. I'd pull his beard toward me and kiss him like the sky was breaking up.

Right now, all I want to do is cry and hope he comes to hold me before I lose it.

Inhaling deeply, his tongue trails his bottom lip. "So...if I rip your clothes off and make love to you out here, we won't get caught?" he asks, still looking at the water.

"N-no."

He shifts his gaze to me again and thunders toward me, slamming his lips on mine and kissing me like it's the first time. Our clothes don't survive their removal. My fuchsia top is ripped off me, his checked shirt loses its buttons revealing his chiseled sweaty chest underneath, and my pants are torn open. This is the dream that keeps me smiling.

He lifts me onto my patio table and fucks me raw. When we're done, he fucks me again, releasing the missed months of passion. We're back, aren't we? He's home.

We sigh in satisfaction after making love for thirty minutes, and rest on the lounge chair, letting the early afternoon sun caress our nude bodies. I missed this, I never realized it but I do.

His fingers snake through my hair and play with it, twirling pieces around his fingers. "I saw what happened on the news." He kisses my forehead gently.

I sigh. "It's been a heck of a few months." My fingers trace the outlines of his pecks. "What took you so long to come see me?"

His lips are still pressed on my head. "I wasn't sure if I should. Thought you might've gotten back with your husband."

"I'm not really sure what I'm doing in that department." I already know what I'm doing, but chuckle anyway. "I have two years to make that decision."

"Can I tell you my decision?" he asks, still twirling my hair.

I nuzzle my head on his sweaty chest. "Mm, please."

"I want to be with you," he says softly.

I don't know what to say, so I smile, kissing his chest and adjusting my head on it, again.

I want to be with you, too, Silas.

He swallows thickly. "And, uh, I came because of that. And you talked about your house in Malibu so much I thought I'd give it a look."

"How did you even get in?"

He lifts a shoulder. "Knocked a few times, then decided to just wait out here. The latch on your side door is broken, y'know."

"Mhm, broke it by accident four years ago when I pushed the door open too roughly," I say, tracing the contours of his abs. "What have you been up to?"

"Fixed up the house a bit." He shrugs, clicking his tongue. "Thinking about you too much."

"I've been thinking about you too much, too."

"It's really good to see you," he says, dropping my hair and hugging me.

God, I'm so happy I might cry. For three months I've done nothing but cry because I was sad. Because my entire life was uplifted and came crumbling down. Taking in the new year shouldn't mean finding out your father-in-law tried to have you killed. Or an eminent divorce with your husband.

No, I should have been celebrating the year to come with my husband and his stupid family while dreaming of the days I'd make up with mine. Jack would be so proud of me. I just know he would.

Having Silas here is the happy ending I didn't know I wanted. Us living in my house on the water with nothing but clear skies and the sound of crashing waves. There's still that silence he loves. We can make this work.

I giggle, squeezing him back. "It's good to see you, too, Silas."

"Wanna take a shower, then have some lunch?"

"I'd like that." I kiss his lips as sweat covers our bodies. His upper lip is drenched. Clearly, he hasn't been in hot weather in a little while. I don't care, I find it incredibly sexy how soaked we are but aren't moving.

"You have actual food in your fridge and not the vegan stuff you said you ate, yeah?" he asks, gripping my hair.

I giggle and maneuver myself on top. "Yes, I have real food." Ugh, it's actually kind of gross how sweaty we are when our junk touches. "I really need to shower."

"Mm," he says, pulling my breasts to his lips.

"Hold that thought, we'll continue this in a second." I get off him and pick up our clothes.

He grabs my ass roughly and picks up his jeans and ripped shirt, then our shoes. I don't even have to look around to know some trespassing paparazzi just had a field day taking our picture. I don't care, really. The world has seen me naked in my films, and to see me naked doing my favorite thing in real life is an even bigger turn-on. I'm back. I'm finally back to being myself.

"You ain't got much furniture," he comments on the minimalistic modern style we have.

"We're not pack rats."

Silas' house has so many knickknacks, books, and picture frames crowding every inch of his house. It's distracting. Even when it's clean it looks dirty because it's cluttered.

"I gotta lotta shit." He chuckles. "Think I can bring it all here?"

I stop walking, slowly turning to him because I don't mind the thought of having his things here. But I do mind clutter. "Or we can leave it there and only bring your necessities. Use your place as our little getaway?"

"I like that idea."

I giggle and lead him to the washroom in the master bedroom that's on the first floor. We renovated and made the study and spare bedroom into one large room, adding a walk-in closet and en suite to it as well. The large bedroom that was originally the master bedroom, is now the library and office for us. This is the room in the house I love escaping to and sitting on the balcony to watch the sunrise. My house is beautiful, I know this, magazines know this, but clearly, Silas isn't used to this type of minimalist style. He'll get used to it, I'm sure.

I turn the shower on, touching the water as his hands touch my hips. He doesn't wait for the water to warm, he lifts me and puts me down in the shower. Our shower sex in the cabin was my absolute favorite, I can't wait to explore it in mine where we actually have room and no finicky knobs.

Water washes over us and his kiss deepens, sending throbs through me. Fuck, I wanted this so badly for so long. He's that itch that I needed to scratch.

His kisses move from my lips to my neck, then graze my nipples before he suckles on them. I let out a moan, and I can tell he likes it from the smirk on his face. I've gone down on him many times before, but he's never licked me. And I think he's about to do it.

The second his kisses hit my navel, he gets to his knees and parts my legs. Oh, God, his tongue feels electric. The way he teases me with it causes me to grab the hair on top of his head and pull. A growl rumbles through his chest and he squeezes my thighs. Whenever Adrien ate me out, he liked it when I was on my knees and he ate me from behind. The only reason I made sure to wax my asshole was so Adrien wouldn't be disgusted if I wasn't fully bald down there.

I lift my leg and rest it on Silas's shoulder, making it easier for him to make me climax. It doesn't take long, either, I squeal and writhe under his touch, squeezing his head with my hands and forcing him off me. Savagely, he whips me around and shoves his dick in me.

He thumps quickly and cums as quickly as I did. Doesn't bother me, either, my legs feel like rubber right now. Plus, we went three times in the last hour. He has me pinned to the tiled wall. Our moans move through my quiet house, enveloping us in the lost months of lust. There's the energy I missed.

He bites my shoulder and exhales deeply. I like the silence between us. It shows how comfortable we can be. But sometimes, I want to talk, and today is one of those days. I feel like a chatterbox.

I giggle, kissing him passionately. "Mm-Mm-Mm, it's good to have you back."

He gropes my ass. "Yeah."

Adrien wouldn't say anything and it's been eating away at me. "What happened after I left?"

"Mm," he grunts, letting the water wash over him.

"I heard gunshots and then I heard nothing."

He squirts body wash onto my loofah and moves it around his chest and stomach. As disturbing as the scar is, it's kind of sexy right now—Nope, back to the task at hand.

"Your husband was pleading for his life, but I called the cops from his phone instead."

My gaze flickers from one eye to the next. "What about the men he hired?"

He starts to wash me with the loofah. "Story for another day, darling."

"Did you have to shoot anyone?" I ask, his dealings with the Belizzos is intriguing, and an attribute I know very little about.

"Like I said, story for another day," he repeats, holding my chin and kissing me.

I desperately want to know the truth about what happened after I escaped, but maybe it is better to leave those stones turned over and buried. For now.

"How's Marlow doing?" I ask, turning in his grasp.

He starts washing me some more, groping my soapy breasts. "Couple fractured ribs and she's been walking with a limp, but she's fine." He chuckles. "Been milking it the last few months so I'd keep giving her treats."

I grew a liking to Marlow over the weeks I was there. "Must be happy to be home?"

"Didn't like me leaving too much."

I close my eyes and step under the water. "Who's she staying with?"

He moves my hair to the side."Marty's watching her."

"How long do you plan on staying?"

"How long do you plan on having me?" he asks, kissing my cheek.

I slide my hands around his waist. "If I had it my way, we'd be doing nothing but fucking all day every day until we get sick of each other."

He chuckles, kissing me lightly and pushing me under the falling water with him.

We shower in silence, basking in each other's presence like we used to do at his home. He likes the silence. It's like we're back where we left off, minus the fear of wondering what was going to happen to me.

I get out of the shower before him so he can rinse off. Fuck, I'm starving. Since he got me eating meat again, I've been less hungry than I used to be. Which is beneficial but a downfall for the scale. But I'm starving right now because I skipped breakfast. The interview made me very nervous. And when I get nervous on a full belly, bile builds up. There's no telling what interviewers could ask or what I would say. I could get mad and say something I'll regret, and I didn't want that happening. It's done. I can finally breathe.

He wipes his eyes and looks at me through the reflection of the mirror. "Mind getting me my deodorant since you're out of the shower?"

I wrap the towel around me, wringing out my hair. "Sure, where is it?"

"Somewhere in the bag," he says.

I find his bag in the dining room. The shower is still on, I hear the water pelting the glass from Silas standing under it. He doesn't have much in his bag aside from clothes, books, and a cell phone. The plastic is still on the box and the bill is crumbled beside it. Did he do this for me? So we could talk every day if he's not around? I remember Billy talking about cell phone towers being added to Silas' side of the river.

Deodorant. Deodorant. Where the fuck did he put it?

I rummage through the opening and hit something metallic. I don't even have to pull it out to know it's one of his guns. Why the fuck did he bring this?

My hands start to shake thinking maybe this is for me. No. No, no. Silas wouldn't do that, he was trying to protect me. Maybe he still is. He brought this to protect us. That's what it is.

I open the side pockets and find nothing in one of them, and half a bag of chips in the other with a crumbled piece of paper. Curiosity strikes since it looks like there's blood on the paper.

Why are you opening it, you idiot?!

I adjust the towel around me and open the blood-stained letter. I gasp and a whimper escapes my lips.

Silas, It's not over yet. I need you to finish what you started before you get us all killed. Do it and your freedom will be granted.

Colm.

My hands are shaking so violently, I can barely read the letter. Oh, God, was I played all this time? It was Silas, wasn't it? He tried to kill me and failed so he pretended to save me. I slept with the guy that tried to kill me. Jesus fucking, FUCK!

"Parker? You find it?" Silas calls, making his way to me as he runs a towel through his hair.

I don't say anything and turn slowly, holding the paper in my hand. He stops and meets my eyes which are welling with tears. He doesn't have to say anything, the shame is all over his face.

"What is this?" I ask, my voice is shaky and low.

He looks down at his calloused hand, picking at it with his thumb. I want to be terrified right now, I want to run and scream, but fuck my sick and twisted mind can't ignore how tasty he looks right now. The towel is draped over his shoulder, water is rolling down his chest and getting lost in his slight chubby. Why do the bad guys always have to look so good?

He still doesn't say anything as he pokes at his callous. Everything is running through my mind and yet, there's nothing I can think about other than the fact I was wrong, so terribly wrong.

His eyebrows raise to look up at me. That shame is wiped right off his face and is replaced with a devious grin. His hand drops to his side as he takes a step toward me. I reciprocate and step back until my ass hits the dinette in the kitchen.

He's standing before me, that smirk still spread to his lips and takes the paper from my hand. I don't know what to do. I'm literally frozen right now. I'm telling my limbs to move but they won't. I'm forcing myself to scream, but I can't. Why can't I scream?

His hands lift and caress my cheek, wiping away a tear before he holds my head in his hands. His lips touch mine, but I don't kiss back. He leaves them there, his hands slithering to my neck. His thumbs caress my throat and rest there.

"Seems like I've got some explaining to do," he says into my parted lips. His accent is gone. What the fucking fuck? "But now's not the time, is it?"

"Silas?" I whimper.

A chuckle leaves him, his lips still grazing mine.

I shudder, inhaling his breath. My moment has come. All my fear and all my troubles are officially over.

It's my time. Isn't it?